Bony and the White Savage

Bony Novels by Arthur Upfield:

Bony and the White Savage

ARTHUR W. UPFIELD

ETT IMPRINT
Exile Bay

Chapter One

The Homing Prodigal

Karl Mueller was an old-timer in the deep south-west of Western Australia. His parents had migrated from Hamburg to settle north of Albany, and there Karl and his sister were born. Karl's sister had married well, and with her children lived in Albany. Karl, however, lacked ambition. All he had inherited was his father's love of the sea and his mother's love of the mountains and the trees and the farm animals.

For twenty-odd years Karl had worked for the Jukes who owned a farm and large grazing lease a few miles inland from Rhudder's Inlet, and almost within sight of the famous Leeuwin Lighthouse which is said to signpost the approach to Australia's Front Door. Now fifty years old, he looked less than forty, being nobbly rather than stout, blond of hair and blue of eyes, possessed of one virtue, loyalty, and one vice, alcohol.

Every year he departed to spend the Christmas and New Year with his sister and family in Albany, returning always in the first week of January. He had a great aversion to spending money on rail and road services, and invariably walked both ways, and no aversion to spending money on booze and on presents for those whom he held in high regard, including his employer's wife. He tramped the hundred-and-fifty-odd miles, keeping as close to the coast as rivers and inlets permitted, the western half of the journey lying over unsettled country of forest and gully and stream.

For the record, this year he left Albany on 2 January, and on the evening of the ninth he made early camp beside a long disused logging track. All this day he had tramped up and over the tree-massed hills bordering the Southern Ocean, fording one river and, without removing his boots, tramping across the streams and sluggish water-gutters. He had greeted in his open simple fashion particular trees and rocks he remembered from previous journeys, and in three days he had not passed a house.

Making camp in this quarter of Australia at this time of year is no chore to men like Karl Mueller. He chose to sleep in the lee of a robust bush, and instinctively built his small fire on clear ground. He boiled water in a quart pot, brewed tea, added a dash of rum, and, having supped, emptied the residue of the tea upon the embers of the fire. He unrolled his swag hard against the bush that he would not be disturbed by the moonlight, and having smoked his pipe and downed another double nobbier of rum, laid himself on the blankets, shut his eyes and slept. He was awakened, so he thought, by someone humming a tune.

That anyone should be humming a tune in the middle of the night in this wildly virgin country was so unusual that Karl attributed it to the dwindling effects of the many bottles of rum he had consumed during his holiday. He lay there in the shadow of the bush beside the track, thinking he would like a snort but remembering there was but one left in the last bottle, and deciding to reserve that for breakfast.

The night was as silent as the inside of a possum's nest in winter, and the sound of a stick snapping on the leaf-and-debris covered track could not be ignored. Karl now knew that someone was coming along the track and humming the tune of 'Onward Christian Soldiers'.

That was when the nightmare began, the creeping warning of terror. Karl was lying parallel with the track, and without raising his head he could see beyond his feet the figure of the man coming from Albany way. The clear moonlight fell full upon him, and his face Karl had hoped never to see again. He was six feet tall, and would scale at least two hundred pounds. He walked with the peculiar gait which Karl remembered, head up, chest out, shoulders well back, like one accustomed to being stared at and admired. The beret was worn at a rakish angle, and the moonlight glittered on the ornament, or badge, worn at the front.

One part of Karl's mind claimed it must be the booze that brought about this visitation; and yet another part warned him to remain still and try not to sever the ropes binding him. The man advanced, waving his left hand to the beat of the tune he hummed. In the other hand he carried a suitcase. When beside Karl, when about to pass him, Karl gazed up at his face, and it was, indeed, the man whom no one wanted ever to remember. The face was large, the flesh slack under the eyes and about the mouth. The forehead was broad, but the chin was weak. The hands were broad and fingers were stubby and powerful. The left hand still beat the time of the tune, and as the hummer was about to pass Karl the humming was interrupted to permit the voice to say:

"Onward, you bastards, onward."

The widely-spaced, black eyes fixed their gaze directly forward, failing to notice the victim of nightmare lying within a yard of the large feet. Another stick snapped, and the ropes about Karl snapped. The terror waned, and he swung his body over to lie on his chest and gaze along the track to see the figure emerge from shadow into moonlight, and beyond the moonlight again into shadow, and vanish.

"Must be having a touch of the horrors," he told himself, and drawing a blanket up and over his head, slept dreamlessly until sun-up.

Karl tossed the blanket aside and sat on the ground-sheet. The bush was dark green and mountainous upon his left, and the old logging track passed close to his right side. Yes, that was where he had seen the man with the heavy white face, the wide shoulders, the thick legs with their majestic tread, and the old tune hummed as he had hummed it so many years agone. Marvin Rhudder, rapist, basher, gaol-bird, had passed by on the moonlit track in the dead centre of the hours of night.

It wasn't real this morning of bright sunshine, when the kookaburras in a nearby gully were chuckling, and a butcherbird on a near branch was looking at him with his head to one side. What tricks the booze will play on a man, lifting him up and then dumping him like a sack in the bush to have a bout of the horrors. Karl stood, stretched, relaxed. He didn't feel good and he didn't feel bad. This day he would be home again.

The remainder of the water in his canvas-bag he poured into the quart pot and boiled it for a brew of tea. Into the tea he emptied the remainder of the rum, and whilst sipping the concoction and chewing hard biscuits with a sliver of hard cheese, he felt again the doubt that the passing of Marvin Rhudder had been hallucination. Still worrying, he rolled his swag and sat on it while filling his pipe and smoking for fifteen minutes, the while arguing aloud the pros and cons as though the butcher-bird could understand what he was saying.

"Look! The last we heard about this Marvin Rhudder swine is that he's doing time for bashing and raping a woman on a vacant allotment in a Sydney suburb. If it was him last night, then he's out of gaol. If he was heading for home, and he wouldn't be here in the West without going home, he wouldn't of been coming this way from Albany. He'd of been coming down from Timbertown on the milk truck, having come over to the West by train or ship. I can't see him coming home, anyway, not after old Jeff Rhudder swearing a thousand times to shoot him on sight. Naw! Musta been mistook. Musta been a fit of the horrors. I expected 'em, but they didn't come till last night.

"All right! Then let's say it was him. We won't argue how he got here. I got twelve miles to do today to get me home. He's got fourteen or fifteen miles to get him back to the Inlet. He won't be doing that right off, or will he? Could of camped for a spell at the old mill where there's water, and he had none with him, and then branch off south to hit the Inlet right on the coast. Oh, blast it, I musta been mistook."

Karl stood and knocked the dottle from his pipe, stamping it out on the hard ground. He poured the residue of the tea leaves on the now cold fire ashes, just to make sure there lingered not one spark, slung the swag behind a shoulder and strapped the gunny-sack to fall suspended against his chest. Although the contents of the gunny-sack weighed twice as much as the swag, the arrangement gave balance and left both hands and arms free.

Five miles on he could see the site of the old timber mill, nothing of it left save a few uprights once supporting the iron roof, and the battered useless debris littering the banks of a stream which now carried but a narrow flow of water. Karl spent almost an hour reconnoitring before he was assured no one was camped hereabout, and when again on his way he was convinced that the experience of the previous night was a dream.

Even if it hadn't been a nightmare, Marvin Rhudder would have followed the little stream down from the old mill, followed it southward to the Inlet and then along the shore of the imprisoned water to reach his people's homestead. Karl's way was no longer on a track. He trudged up the slopes and down them, and presently he gained the top of a hill from which he could see Rhudder's Inlet all blue and shimmering right to the narrow entrance from the distant Southern Ocean beyond the white dunes. He could see the Rhudder homestead seemingly protected by the coast dunes, a rambling house surrounded by work-sheds, the milking-shed, the stockyards. His home at the Matthew Jukes farm was five miles inland.

Emma Jukes was mixing a cake batter when the dogs began to bark, and the barking became frenzied when she heard Karl Mueller shouting at them. His was a joyful shouting, the joy of a man happy to be home again. Then he was standing just inside the open door of the large kitchen-living-room, smiling broadly at her, and lowering to the floor his swag and gunny-sack.

"Good dayee, Missus! Got home, you see."

Poor Karl! His suit purchased in Albany had been slept in during the journey. His boots were caked with mud and dust. His whiskers were two inches long. His eyes were still bloodshot although now wide and bright.

"And glad to see you, Karl," Emma said. "Have a nice break in Albany?"

"Too true, Missus. Same old joint. Same pubs, same sister and brother-in-law. I got something for you. Hope you like it."

"You have!" Emma Jukes turned to spoon tea into the pot and pour boiling water from the heavy iron kettle. She was small and compact. Her greying brown hair was coiled neatly in a bun at the back of her head. Her brown eyes were alive and excited. Karl untied the mouth of the sack, gazed inside for several tantalizing moments, and brought out a package wrapped in gilt paper. Then, when Emma was looking and waiting, he said bashfully:

"Sort of proving I didn't forget the old farm when I was away."

Emma Jukes removed the wrapping to disclose a small brooch fashioned after a butterfly. For a moment or two she stood looking at the brooch, and Karl waited as though anxious for her verdict. It wasn't the thrill of receiving this present which sent her hastening to a wall mirror, to pin it to her dress. Dear, simple, honest, affectionate Karl. For twenty years he had worked with them and for them, and when their boy was taken by the sea, he had slipped into their hearts. Her eyes were very bright when again she faced him across the table.

"Why, it's just lovely, Karl. How nice of you to think of me."

It always had been like this on the return from his annual bender. No gush. Just plain appreciation in her eyes, and simple happiness in his broad smile at the pleasure he gave. She poured tea and produced small cakes from a tin, and urged him to sit and eat whilst she continued with her mixture. He told her about the sister and the children, and the brother-in-law who was doing fine. He spoke of the various publicans in Albany in a manner as though they were close relations, and afterwards he picked up the heavy gunny-sack and emptied the contents on the floor, displaying together with new boots and new shirts a mass of paperbacks.

"Look at 'em, Missus," he urged Emma. "All good blood-and-gutzers. Look! *Wuthering Heights! Kidnapped! Peyton Place! Blood on the Sand!* The woman at the shop picked 'em out for us. We'll have some sessions now, won't we?"

"They look fine, Karl," agreed Emma. "Now pack them on the sideboard, and go make yourself ready for dinner. Matt has Jack helping him with the milking and things, and Jack'll be wanting to go home tonight."

"Still courtin' Eve?" asked Karl.

"We think so. Now, run along and make yourself tidy."

"By golly, yes," he responded, having glanced at the clock on the mantel. He scooped up the boots and oddments into the sack, picked up the swag, and again at the doorway, turned to say: "See you later, Missus."

When Emma did see him again, he was shaved and showered and dressed as always for the evening in white open-necked shirt and drill trousers. He came in with her husband and a youth of nineteen. Matt Jukes was nearing sixty, and the years had whitened his hair but had not touched his black beard nor dimmed the dark and brilliant eyes. He was stocky and powerful of build, and now he was chuckling at something Karl had told them.

After dinner Karl took the utensils to the wash-bench, and Emma expostulated, saying, "This is still your holiday time." But he came back swiftly with the objection that as she had cooked the dinner it was his job to clean up as he had done for years. And afterwards, as had also been the custom for years, he would be rewarded by Emma reading to him one of his 'blood-and-gutzers'.

The temporary help roared away on his motor-bike back to Timbertown, and Emma tidied up and lit the power lamp suspended from the ceiling. Matt went off to lock up the fowls from the foxes, and when he returned he heard Emma say:

"Something on your mind, Karl? You're very quiet all of a sudden."

Matt sat with them at the table on which Emma had laid out the new books, and without speaking he began to load his pipe. Karl, he thought, looked tired, looked old tonight, and the annual bender wasn't being carried off as stoutly as hitherto. Karl said slowly, wonderingly:

"Yes, there is, Missus. I can't make up me mind if I seen Marvin Rhudder last night or not."

The pipe slipped from Matt's hands to the table-cloth, and Emma uttered a soft gasp of astonishment.

"Yes," Karl repeated. "And I can't make up me mind." They could see the uncertainty and desperation in his soft blue eyes. He could see on their faces the shock, and all the sorrow that had been there thirteen years before. Haltingly he related the experience of the night on the track.

"You sure you saw what you saw, dream or real?" pressed Matt Jukes, his voice hard, his eyes blazing.

"That's what I dreamed or what I saw," answered Karl.

"But would you recognize him after all this time?" Matt argued. "Remember, when he went away he was only a lad, only just turned twenty. He'd be thirty-three now. He'd be different."

The heaviness lifted from Karl Mueller, and he smiled with relief. It was a dream after all. Then the smile vanished, and the weight of memory appeared to crush him into his chair.

"No, I know now it was real," he said. "I remember that as he was passing me he was humming like he used to. He was humming 'Onward Christian Soldiers' like he used to."

Chapter Two

The Timbertown Policeman

Senior Constable Samuel Sasoon was the toughest of the many nuts Timbertown had failed to crack. A superficial survey of Timbertown would lead one to presume that it could not crack a soft-shelled egg, all being nice and quiet and genteel during business hours.

Samuel Sasoon's father had been a tree-faller and sleeper-cutter in the forests of the immense Karri country, inland from the coast, between the Leeuwin Light and Albany. He had the physique of a gorilla; the nimbleness of a dancing master. It was as nothing for him to scale a karri trunk for two hundred feet to lop off the great crown of branches, and cling like a limpet to the beheaded trunk when the crown gave it the ponderous kick at parting, causing the bare trunk to vibrate like a tuning fork. He would ask someone to drive a peeled stick into the ground, anywhere they chose, and then fell the vast trunk exactly upon it. Once he failed. The trunk missed the stick by a couple of yards; he broke down and wept and got himself drunk for a week.

The huge karri trees have killed many men, and continue to do so, but the elder Sasoon was killed by a piece of orange peel on the main street at Timbertown. Young Samuel was then fifteen and showing the promise of his sire's body and feet. Also he was showing his mother's fear of heights and his mother's love of books of which she possessed two: the Bible and *Uncle Tom's Cabin*.

There being an elder brother to carry on the Sasoon tradition, young Samuel pitted himself against human giants in preference to the lords of the forests. He was given his first chance when, among the attractions of a visiting carnival, there was the usual boxing booth, with the usual gorillas issuing invitations to step inside and try one's science. Having no science to try out, young Sasoon stepped inside and flattened the lot one after another, and was at once promoted to head-man by the proprietor.

For two years he remained with the show, travelling all over the State, and then on impulse he joined the Western Australia Police Department. Meanwhile, the timber mills operating in the vicinity of Timbertown had increased, and the population of tough nuts had multiplied to such an extent that the force there had to be doubled. Eventually, instead of re-doubling, the Brass decided to send young Samuel Sasoon to help out.

Constable Sasoon had a way with him, and the reach to put it into effect. A brawl outside the hotel or the dance hall was ever a magnet drawing Constable Sasoon. He would advance upon the brawlers. Then on impact he would seize a man with one hand and another with the other and crash their heads together. Dropping them like wet sacks, he would seize another couple and repeat the process, and so on, until he was on the far side of the crowd. He would then pause to admire the stars or something before returning and, should there be any adventurous spirit lingering on the scene ... but after the trial run there never was.

He married Emma Jukes's best friend, and despite the fact that he never charged a man with being d. and d., he was promoted to Senior Constable. The years tamed him, but not much, and experience broadened his mind as the boxing tent had broadened his shoulders.

There was nothing beyond the ordinary about Timbertown. There was Main Street fronted by stores and shops, the Post Office, the Court House, the Council Chamber, with the Hospital and the Police Station down a side street. The nearest mill was half a mile out of town, and hard against the terminus of the railway. Flowering gum-trees shadowed the streets, and the gardens around the houses were always bright.

He was working on a case to prosecute at court when he heard Matt Jukes in the outer office giving details about a car registration to the constable on duty, and, without leaving his chair, called to Matt to come in when he'd concluded his business. A minute or two later, Matt entered the inner office to be greeted with a cheerful grin and the invitation to take a pew.

"Got an item of news, Matt," Sasoon said, reaching for tobacco and papers. "Came down this morning. How's things?"

He was relaxed, in his shirt-sleeves. His sandy hair was now scant, but his grey eyes had lost nothing of their youth and joy of living. Matt Jukes was older, shorter, as tough, and his dark eyes had lost nothing of youth either.

"All right, Sam. Been a bit undecided what foot to stand on, though, since Karl came home from Albany," replied Matt, now looking troubled. "Can't make anything of it. Can't make up my mind yet if Karl was having a nightmare or not."

"Never knew he had nightmares, Matt. The horrors, yes." Jukes sighed, hesitated, then burst forth.

"Don't like thinking about bad times. Don't want 'em brought back to mind. But there's Karl camped a few miles east of the old Stoney Creek mill. The moon's high and him in shadow, and he thinks he saw Marvin Rhudder walk past, coming back home."

"Thinks!" stressed Sasoon, stubbing his cigarette. His eyes had lost their customary benignity.

"Still thinks he did and he didn't. Me and Emma thinks he did because Karl says, as Marvin was passing him, he was humming 'Onward Christian Soldiers'. Ever since, I've been on Ocean Ridge watching the Rhudders' place through glasses, and I've not seen Marvin about, and the others haven't done anything out of routine."

"How long's this been going on?" Sasoon asked, and hearing someone enter the outer office, left his chair to close the inner door.

"Well, Karl got back yesterday week."

"You been watching for a week?"

Matt nodded, and returned to the chore of filling his pipe. There was slight wonderment in Sasoon's eyes when he asked:

"Why the hell didn't you ring me up about it?"

"Well, what for? If it was Marvin, then he must be out of gaol, he must be off licence and able to come home. No crime in coming home, is there?"

Sasoon selected a document from a tray and again read it. For a period he pondered, before looking across the desk at Matt. He said, as though carefully choosing his words:

"What do you really think, Matt? Did Karl see the feller, or was sight of him due to the booze?"

"I put the odds in favour of his having seen Marvin."

"You mean in reality?"

"Yes. I reminded Karl that Marvin had been away thirteen years, and that he'd be much older. It was the old habit of humming hymns that threw Karl off balance."

"Karl describe him to you?"

"Yes. Marvin was wearing a good suit. It was black or dark-grey. He was carrying a suitcase and nothing else. And he wore a beret with a brooch or ornament at the front."

"Ah." Sasoon almost breathed. "What was that like?"

"Looked like silver. A cross inside a circle."

"Feller must be mad," Sasoon said, stressing the adjective, and before Matt could query who must be mad, Sasoon picked up the telephone, and called for Bunbury 10. Matt heard him say:

"Senior Constable Sasoon asking if Inspector Hudson's available. All right. Please. Sasoon here, sir. Reference your memo 1761–143. I have grounds to believe that the person has entered this district. He was seen with the bookmaker's lucky charm pinned to his beret. Yes. That's correct, sir. Yes, he must have doubled back. Very well, sir, I'll be here."

Sasoon replaced the receiver and stared at Matt, and Matt stared back and waited, silently.

"Did you bring Emma to town?" asked the policeman, and Matt shook his head.

Sasoon again lifted the receiver and this time asked for Timbertown 189. Now Matt frowned because this was his own house number. Then he was hearing:

" 'Day, Emma! Nice day, eh! Good to hear your voice. Too right, it's your old friend. Now listen and no gossip. Of course, Else is O.K. Yes, I know that. Look, is Karl handy? Good! Bring him to the phone, will you?"

No sound other than the constable in the outer office using the typewriter, until Sasoon spoke again.

"Yeh, it's me, Karl. Been having a few words with Matt here. Now listen and name no names. That night you camped the other side of the mill, remember? Where d'you reckon he'd turn off from your course? Oh, then he'd cross Rhudder's Creek. How's she running? Pretty low, eh? Muddy both sides? Well now, there could be a lot in what you dreamed that night, see? You stick around with Emma till Matt gets home. Yes, just stick around. Matt won't be long."

Sasoon replaced the instrument. Again he meditated, then he said with grit in his voice:

"Wait! Breckoff!"

The constable entered, a robust rather good-looking young man.

"Tom, run out to Lew's camp, and see if he can hunt up a couple of trackers. Don't bring 'em in. Have them standing by at short call. Lew'll understand we have a job for them. Tell him we want the best."

"All right, Senior."

"And, Breckoff, the boss will be down here this afternoon. You know what he's like about tunics, and dress in general."

"I haven't forgotten what he said last time, Senior," and with a faint grin Breckoff departed. Sasoon waited until the door was shut.

"Well, that's that," he said to Matt Jukes. "Eight days that swine's been home and you tell me now. All the police in South Australia, Victoria and New South Wales are looking for him, and he's right under our noses. You didn't go down to the house asking for him, did you?"

"No. I watched for him from the Ridge, as I said."

"You didn't see him through the glasses?"

"Not a glimpse. I told you we couldn't be sure about him coming back. If I had been sure, I'd have gunned for him."

"I can believe that, Matt." Sasoon stood, towering over the seated grazier. "Matt, you've been tried pretty sorely, but what's past has got to be kept past. Now you know me and I know you. I know that once you promise anything you'll abide by it. You promise me you won't go

14

gunning for him."

The policeman stared down into the wide dark eyes now aflame with hot rage and, because he himself could seldom retain anger for longer than a quarter-hour, he marvelled that Matt could continue to hate for thirteen years. Matt Jukes had in him the stuff of long and vicious feuds.

"Well," Sasoon insisted. "You promise to keep the peace, or I'll lock you up."

Matt Jukes bounced to his feet and, because he was a foot shorter, glared upward at the policeman.

"You'd lock me up?" he yelled. "You?"

"Yair, me. And if I couldn't do it all by myself I'd call on Emma and Else to help me. They'd help me quick and lively." Sasoon sat again, and motioned Matt to do likewise. "Now look, Matt, this business is bigger than you got any idea of. The Law is goin' to give you and me and Emma all the satisfaction we've ever wanted from Marvin Rhudder. Yes, the Law is going to do the gunning. You seen Luke Rhudder?"

"He came home five days ago. Didn't call in, but I seen him from the Ridge."

"Calling the Legions to Rome, Matt. Now what I'm going to tell you, you keep under the hat. Marvin has made a fatal mistake. He raped a woman and murdered a bookmaker. Now we know that in New South Wales, where's he's been operating for thirteen years, rape is thought to be the naughty ebullience of the teenager, and murder is considered the impulsive act of a sick man. But, Matt, Marvin committed his last criminal assault on a woman and his first murder in the State of South Australia, where murderers are hanged."

"So what?" queried Matt Jukes.

"No matter where he's picked up. Marvin gets extradited to South Australia."

"If he's picked up," argued Matt. "If you think all you got to do is run down to the homestead and arrest Marvin with no more trouble than serving a summons, you'll think nothing. He's not lying on the couch in the lounge or sleeping in the best bedroom. He's holed up in a cave, and you know there's more holes and caves to every mile of coast than there's stars in the sky. The only chance to pick him up, as you call it, is to pick him off with a rifle fitted with telescopic sights. A ruddy army of police couldn't pick him up."

"You talk sense, Matt," admitted Sasoon. "It's going to be a problem, but it is a police problem. Eight days he's been home, that is if he stayed at home eight days. Might have stayed home only one night, and now where could he be? As you point out, we don't raid the Rhudder homestead like a two-up school in a city."

"You sent for the abos," Matt said, adding, with regained calm: "That's something."

"Routine, Matt. By now every station in W.A. will be given the good oil about Marvin. Now you go home and stay close. No more going off to the Ridge and watching. You watch out for Emma."

"Emma's all right. She's afraid of no man."

"Man," echoed Sasoon. "Marvin Rhudder isn't a man. He's a throw-back to a prehistoric monster."

Chapter Three

Bony Takes Charge

It was Monday evening and a quiet night in Timbertown, and having inspected the few passengers who had left the train from Perth, Sam Sasoon was taking his ease in the front room of the Police Quarters, reading a novel whilst his wife sewed and the large black cat purred. The window was wide open, and there entered the normal sounds of a quiet town until footsteps sounded on the concrete path from the front gate.

"Could be him," Sasoon said, and put aside his book.

"Funny time to arrive," observed Elsie Sasoon, glancing at the mantel clock. She was stout, blonde, age difficult to assess. "Now, don't worry, Sam. You did everything possible; you know you did."

Sam rose to answer the knocking on the door, and in the passage he could see, beyond the fly-screen, the man revealed by the outside light. He was slim, and he was wearing a cool-looking grey suit.

"Senior Constable Sasoon?" he asked, his voice softly distinct and without accent. "The name is Bonnar, Nathaniel Bonnar."

"Been expecting you," Sasoon said. "Please come in."

He led the way to the sitting-room and his wife rose to meet the visitor. Her first impression was of a man from a tropical film. Her second improved the first. Then she felt pleasure when he bowed to her, and wonderment when she found herself caught in the net of his startling blue eyes.

"I am Nat Bonnar, *pro tem.*," she was informed. "I've been looking forward to meeting both of you."

"We thought you would arrive early this afternoon," Sasoon said, and his wife added her contribution with the usual and normal question: "Have you had dinner?"

"Yes, I put up at the hotel. What delayed me was the karri trees beside the road. They are tremendous. I feel I have left Australia on the far side of the world."

"You love trees, I can see, Mr Bonnar. Would you like a cup of tea?"

"When my wife asks me for a little extra money, I can resist," Bonnar said. "Not for long, of course. But when she asks if I would like a cup of tea I do not resist for a fraction of a second."

"One of our mob," Sasoon said cheerfully. Elsie Sasoon smiled her appreciation and left for her kitchen; Bonnar was invited to be comfortable and smoke. Sasoon was not at ease, for he knew who this Bonnar was and the assignment given him.

"I've been told that not far from Timbertown an old-time settler found the hollow trunk of a karri tree which must have fallen a century or so ago, and that inside the trunk he built a floor and made of it a two-storied house. Was I taken for a sucker?"

"No," replied the policeman, now discovering that the depression of the last weeks was lifting. "A feller was out looking for his cows, seven of them. It was wet weather and he found 'em inside the trunk of a standing tree. It was big enough for him to have his milking and dairy equipment in there too. You've come to the right place to see real trees."

"True enough, and I haven't lived in a sand desert all my life. By the way, here are my identity papers. Inspector Hudson told you by telephone of my coming, I take it."

"That's right, sir. He didn't mention your real name, though. Not on the phone."

"It was decided I should assume an alias. It has also been worked out with a verifiable background that I am the manager of a pastoral property in the Murchison District. I am now on a holiday tour and hope to see something of the country and do a little fishing. It has been suggested that a Mr Matthew Jukes might put me up as a paying guest."

"That could be arranged I'm sure, sir."

"Did you know Jukes's son, Ted, who was drowned, and his daughter, Rose, who married a store executive and now lives in Geraldton?"

Mrs Sasoon who came in with a supper-tray answered for her husband.

"Oh, yes, we know all of them. Sam and I belong to this south-west. The Brass wanted Sam to take promotion to another station more than once, but this is our country."

"Then you would be aware of the crime committed against Rose, née Jukes, many years ago?"

"That's so," replied Sasoon. "No charge was laid, and there was no official action, and no publicity."

"So I understand. Well, in support of my spurious background, I have a letter of introduction to Matthew Jukes from his daughter. How far can I take them into my confidence to secure complete co-operation?"

"All the way, sir."

"Good! Now from this moment I am Nathaniel Bonnar, from up-country on a holiday. You may call me Nat. And relax. I have read a summary of what took place at the conference in Manjimup, at which you were present. I am familiar, therefore, with the proposition you put up and which was overruled, and I can say that I feel sure you were right and the Brass were wrong." Inspector Bonaparte accepted a second cup of tea.

"The broad plan of operations I insisted upon before consenting to accept this assignment is this. But first let me summarize the position as it is. Following a series of sex crimes in Sydney over a period of thirteen years, Marvin Rhudder seems to have wanted to tour in stolen cars. He came to a place called Elton in South Australia, and there represented himself to a church minister as a theological student on holiday. The minister invited him to be his guest. He actually preached on two occasions, and borrowed money from the minister's wife.

"At the end of two weeks, he was popular in Elton, and it was at the beginning of the third week that he waylaid and ravished a woman one dark night. On the Wednesday night following this crime, he waited outside the garage of a bookmaker returning from the races at Gawler. He bashed the bookmaker, got away with somewhere about fifteen hundred pounds, and bolted in the minister's car. The car was subsequently found near Mildura, over the border in Victoria.

"Marvin Rhudder's prints were found on three parts of the car body, but not, of course, on the steering-wheel. It was taken for granted that he had abandoned the car on his rush journey back to Sydney, and that at that point he did not know he had killed the bookmaker. The day following the abandonment of the car, he must have learned of the murder from the press and the radio, and would also know later on that the police were seeking a man in connexion with it. At no time has the murderer's name been published.

"Abandoning the car at Mildura was clever, for this led the police towards Sydney. Rhudder, however, doubled back to Port Pirie where he signed on a ship taking horses to India. He left the ship at Albany on 3 January when thousands of policemen were hunting for him in Sydney.

"Now this is where it comes close to us," Bony continued. "On the night of 9–10 January the man Karl Mueller saw him in the bright moonlight. Eight days later Matthew Jukes almost casually mentions it to you, knowing nothing to associate Rhudder with murder. Before that day, you also knew nothing of Rhudder being wanted for murder or any other crime, due to the fact that everyone thought he had run back to Sydney. The genesis of the report, which reached you that day Jukes mentioned Mueller's doubts, was the delayed discovery of his prints in the shipping office at Port Pirie.

"He had been home eight days, when you knew he was there. You acted with shrewdness, and Inspector Hudson admits that you were opposed to the course of action on which he insisted. You went to Rhudder's Inlet and there inquired after the son Marvin, and told them that he was suspected of being concerned with the Elton murder. As you anticipated, results were nil. Further, you were opposed to police action, like an organized raid and search, because of the extraordinarily difficult terrain where Rhudder could stay in hiding. You said that, where an army would fail, one man with a tracker could dig him out, and you suggested that you be the man. Instead, and I think they were wise because you are known, they have sent me.

"It is now 27 January and Rhudder has been home, perhaps, for seventeen days. He could have left for a far-away place at any time during the period, so that I may have to hunt for a man who isn't there to locate. Unless you or Matthew Jukes gained evidence that he's still there."

"Nothing of recent date," said Sasoon, obviously pleased by Bony's support. "To get home Rhudder had to cross the main stream into the Inlet. He left his boot-tracks on the mud either side. I took an aborigine there, and I made plaster casts of the tracks. The aborigine was definite about those tracks."

"Definite! Meaning?"

"Quite sure they were Marvin Rhudder's tracks, having remembered the manner of his walking in the early days. They don't forget things like that."

"Go on, more, please," urged Bony, and then aside to Mrs Sasoon: "Do forgive us for talking shop at this hour."

"Following my instructed visit to the Rhudder homestead, I had Lew and another tracker camped a bit off an old track from Albany, just to check if Marvin should break back that way. They report every morning, and so far he hasn't. He could go west to the railheads at Nannup and Augusta, and there police are on their toes. He hasn't come north unless he kept to the forest. Although we've done what we can to close him in, there's plenty of escape routes for anyone born hereabouts."

Sasoon fell silent whilst watching Bony make one of his dreadful cigarettes. He was recharging his pipe when Bony said:

"Your visit to the homestead could have resulted in blurring a clear picture. It is probable that, until you went there, his people would think that the bad egg had turned up having been released from gaol. He would know he was wanted for murder, and would tell them he had broken the condition of his parole and must lie low. I, for one, wouldn't blame his parents for giving sanctuary to him. Then, when you told them he was wanted in connexion with the S.A. murder and having given him sanctuary they would feel obliged to continue. Both before and after your visit, knowing he was wanted for murder, I believe he would stand fast and not chance apprehension. What were the impressions gained at your visit?"

"I've thought about it quite a lot," Sasoon began after a pause. "We've never been real friendly with them like with the Jukes, but we've known them all our lives, and when I've had to call on Government business they've always welcomed me. I didn't like the job, and I was put to disadvantage. I was invited to afternoon tea on the veranda. There was the old man, Jeff Rhudder, who's a cripple with sciatica, his wife, his next son, Luke and his youngest son, Mark. With the family for many years has been a Mrs Stark and her daughter, Sadie. Sadie grew up with the Rhudder children as had the two by Matt Jukes. All went to school together, played pirates and all that.

"As you said just now, about not blaming the parents if Marvin was wanted only for evading the terms of his licence, I wouldn't blame them for helping him to keep holed up. But there's this to it. Many times since his son cleared out after what he done to Rose Jukes, old Jeff has said he'd shoot him like a dog if ever he went back home. They've been keeping tabs on Marvin through a lawyer in Sydney, and I think, or did think, that Jeff Rhudder would carry out his threat. He's that kind of man.

"Now for what you asked. Up to the time I went down there, I think Jeff didn't know Marvin was home. When I left, I think he was suspicious that the others did know, all of them, including Mrs Stark and her daughter. He said something to Luke like 'what did you come home for without the wife and kids?', and there was emphasis on the word 'did'. Every one of 'em denied having seen Marvin since he left home years ago."

"Luke, then, is married and not living at home?"

"That's so. He left home a couple of days after Marvin left. Went to Perth and got himself a job, did pretty well at it, and was married five years back to a nice enough girl, we think."

"When did Luke come down?"

"Three days after Karl Mueller saw Marvin in the night. Been home ever since. I could be wrong, but I think the women sent for him."

"The situation could be worse," Bony decided. "Inspector Hudson says that at this time the Rhudders would believe the police had no firm suspicion that Marvin had returned. Do you agree with that?"

"Yes. Yes, I do. They could have no cause to think otherwise. I was careful to give the impression that I was making a routine inquiry about their son's latest crime committed two thousand miles away. I expressed regret at having to trouble them so sorely, and really felt regret too."

Glancing at the mantel clock, Bony saw the time, and asked for information about the road south to the Jukes's homestead. He was told that the road wasn't good for fast travelling, that it wound down and up steep slopes for seven miles, and then eight miles of better grades, making fifteen miles in all. Should do the journey in under the hour. On from Jukes for four and a half miles would take him to the Rhudder homestead. There were no intervening farms save two on the outskirts of Timbertown.

He was informed that the Jukes were not on a telephone party-line, and this gave him satisfaction. Then he arranged procedure by which he could contact Sasoon, and Sasoon him, and with this understanding he rose to leave.

"It has been a pleasant evening, and thank you for the supper," he said to Elsie Sasoon, and to her husband: "So far you have come out favourably with the top brass, Sam. If Marvin is still down there, I'll pluck him out of it like pulling a feather from a fowl."

Sam Sasoon escorted the visitor to the front gate, and on rejoining his wife, said, smiling broadly:

"Well, what d'you know."

Chapter Four

One Tree Farm

Passing the second farm from Timbertown, the road became a rough track, winding and often steeply graded. Onward, Bony found himself in what any stranger would accept as a primeval forest. From the floor of green bracken and fern rose the jarrahs and cedarwoods, widely spaced, as the best of them had long since been gathered to the mills. The sunlight was beaming between their limpid crowns to cast green-gold pathways on the bracken, and, at this time of day, to polish the creamy grey-blue trunks of enormous karri trees.

On the green floor it was cool and completely still. The wind was blowing at two hundred feet: close to the ground the silence was the silence of a cathedral, with the vocal sounds of the tomtit, the honey-eater, and the lorikeet intruding through the great arched entrance.

Being unable to drive and appreciate this forest, Bony stopped his car, and leaned against it to gaze along the deep fold of a narrow valley. His last assignment had been in the country inland from Shark Bay east of Gladstone, in the arid lands of low scrub and blistering summer heat and searing sunlight. This forest so wonderfully clean of foreign growths wasn't Australia: it was paradise.

The track was a slow one, and there was plenty of time, anyway. It was an hour later that he came to a bar ramp in a wire-fence, and twenty minutes afterwards came to a turn-off sign-posted ONE TREE FARM. Then he was driving towards the one tree and the tiny doll's house his side of it, with other tiny buildings on the far side. The doll's house was confined within a picket-fence, and Bony stopped his car outside the gate and stood entranced by the one tree. There was only the one tree, because fruit-trees and wattles and a couple of cedarwoods beside the track were toys to be bought at a store.

Bony had admired the occasional karri tree beside the road down from Bridgetown; he had been enthralled by the karri trees still standing in the forest, but this one was truly majestic. From behind him a man said:

"Girth at the butt sixty-eight feet. A hundred and seventy-seven feet up to the first branch." Bony's eyes slipped their gaze up the perfect column of blue-grey, up and up with never a halt to disapprove of a blemish, up to the first mighty branch, still upward to encounter the next branches. "Two hundred and eighty-six feet to the top," said the man.

"Proved by the surveyors. Make a dent in the roof if it fell on the house, wouldn't it?"

As Bony's gaze had moved upward like a climbing monkey to the topmost branches, so now it descended down the trunk to the ground. Almost reluctantly, he turned about to the man who had spoken.

"I take it you're Mr Bonnar," said Matt Jukes, plain curiosity in his dark eyes. Without his hat it could be seen he was balding, the greying hair forming a dark halo resting on his ears. "Mrs Sasoon told us you were coming. Come on in and meet the wife."

"Thank you," Bony responded as they shook hands. "Yes, Mrs Sasoon said she would ring you. Gave me a parcel to bring along." He obtained the parcel from the back seat and then halted at the gate in the picket-fence to look back at the tree. "Well, that is a tree of trees. I've seen mountain ash in Gippsland but they're pygmies."

Matt led the way to the rear door of the doll's house, and ushered him into the large living-kitchen-room of a rambling homestead. Emma came to meet the visitor, and in Bony's mind was the thought that Sasoon's wife was large and slow in action, and placid of mind, and this woman was small and vital and quick.

"It's nice to see you, Mr Bonnar," she told him. "Elsie has been raving about you to us. Said you are a friend of our Rose and her husband. Now do sit down, and I'll pour you a cup of tea. It's time for the morning break, anyway. And how did you leave Rose and the children?"

"Mrs Sasoon didn't mention my business?" Bony asked.

"No, she said you were on holiday. D'you take sugar? Just help yourself."

"Thank you." Bony smiled at them, and sipped the tea. "I find myself still a little awed by your karri tree. How old could it be?"

"Probably only a couple of feet shorter when Tasman sailed the water of this coast, and that was 1642," Jukes answered, and there was no evading the pride in his voice. "Biggest tree left standing down this way, and it'll always stand while we're alive. It belongs to us."

"I don't believe that," Bony said charmingly, and added with truth: "You belong to it."

"That's right, Mr Bonnar," Matt agreed, "It's what my father said in his time." He discoursed about recorded giants and told stories of even bigger karri trees which had flourished and fallen before the coming of the white man to stand abashed by the vision of what they must have been when standing. And then when Emma brought up her daughter again, Bony turned his mind to more serious affairs. He said:

"Your buttered scones were delicious, and now that you cannot get them back from me, I will make a confession. Please hear me out before telling me to go. I have here a letter from your daughter which doubtless will tell you a little about me. Several days ago I called on her and her husband. I then explained who and what I am, and the purpose of my intended visit down here, and they were pleased to give me this letter of introduction. Having talked with Constable Sasoon and his wife about you, I am encouraged to take you into my confidence and seek your co-operation in the work I have to do.

"I am supposed to be the manager of a cattle and sheep property away up in the Murchison District. I like fishing, and I am supposed to be a keen amateur photographer and have with me a camera and some pictures to support the claim. Actually, I am a detective-inspector, and actually my assignment is to apprehend a man you know, viz: Marvin Rhudder."

They had both become taut, the woman stilled with her hands in her lap, the man's hands clenched and resting on the table. Bony went on:

"I don't know this part of Australia and the coast, but Sasoon says, and he has pressed the point, that a man holed up down here wouldn't be dug out by an army, and might be by one man acting alone. This is the type of assignment which I have accepted more than once, proving past history in that sometimes it takes an army of detectives to round up one criminal, and other times it demands only one man to corner a gang of crooks.

"In the old-time story-books great detectives were ever the masters of disguise. I am a master in the art of fabricating a fictitious background, and every detail supporting my claim to be the manager of a station in the Murchison District has been firmed in presumed fact, so that anyone wishing to test will find every detail substantiated. Which is why the senior officer at Geraldton and I called on your daughter and explained about the Rhudder problem. They both gladly consented to give me this letter of introduction. Here it is, and here I am.

"And as for the children, Mrs Jukes, I found all four of them just splendid, and when I retire, which I don't suppose I shall, I am going to buy a house like theirs and live in Geraldton."

Jukes and his wife remained quiescent after Bony ceased speaking, and he poured himself another cup of tea and began to roll a cigarette. Matt then said:

"Our Rose wouldn't of told you about what Marvin Rhudder did, I suppose?"

"No. However, Sasoon did hint at some bad trouble years ago when he told me he was sure you would be glad to help me as much as you can."

"I'll help you, too right I'll help," came flooding from Matt Jukes, his eyes blazing and his beard standing out from his chin. "Old Faust traded his soul with the devil for youth, and I'd trade mine for the chance to get my hands on young Rhudder."

"Now, Matt! Please, Matt!" cried Emma, laying a hand over his fist. The man fought for composure and won, but his voice trembled when he spoke again.

"That swine dishonoured our Rose, and he broke his father's heart. Me and old Jeff were boys together. We had our fights and our good times, and we grew up like brothers, and where one had bad fortune, the other always went to his help. We begat children and they all grew up close, playing together, schooling together, adventuring together. You wait till you see old Jeff Rhudder. 'Taint the sciatica what's made him old afore his time. What's made it bad for all of us down here is that we raised Marvin as high as the top of yonder karri, and he went and fell not to the ground but for a mile or more under it. Too true, I'll help you, Mr Bonnar."

"I've been hoping you would, Mr Jukes. Sasoon tells me you know this coast as well as the back of your hand, and that is where we think Marvin is holed up. Or somewhere in the nearby forests. Because of the lapse of time, I've first to be assured he is still down here, and then find him and have him apprehended. And I can expect no assistance from his own people."

"No, you won't get any help from them. Let me tell you about Marvin, as from the beginning. Let's go outside and talk."

Matt rose and strode to the doorway, and Emma cast a look at Bony which was both appealing and encouraging. They sat on a bench against the wall, and again Bony was confronted by the great tree which now dwarfed the picket fence to a line of matching sticks.

"The kids called themselves the Inlet United. There were the three young Rhudders: Marvin, Luke and Mark. There were our two: Ted and Rose. And there was Sadie Stark, the daughter of the woman who's been housekeeping for Mrs Rhudder for many years." Matt paused to light his pipe. "Six of 'em. They was always close; grew up close, you might say, until the explosion."

Emma came from the house and quietly sat next to Bony, and her husband proceeded with the occasional hesitation of the man wanting to choose his words. "Six of 'em, remember. Four boys and two girls. No other children. No neighbours. Marvin was ever the leader, beside being the eldest. What he led 'em into down on the coast made our hair stand on end when we heard tell of it. He saved Sadie from drowning one day and pulled our Ted out from under a sneaker some other time.

"Just imagine those six kids, reared like babies together, going to school on the milk truck to Timbertown, sometimes having a fight, sometimes ganging up to fight the kids in town. We watched 'em growing up, me and Emma and Jeff and his wife, and we were proud of every one of them like they could of been all our own.

"To Marvin learning was as easy as falling out of that karri. He went to High School at Bunbury, and from the High he passed to the Teachers' College up in Perth. Went in for writing stories for the magazines, and could do it without failing anywhere at the College."

Matt stopped to attend to his pipe, and on the other side of Bony, Emma sat with her hands in her lap and in that immobile state he had seen her in before. Her husband sighed, and went on:

"Learnin'! Learnin' wasn't anything to Marvin. Read a poem, shut the book, then recite it. Go to chapel, listen to the sermon, come and repeat what the minister said from first to last. Did his course at the Teachers' College and then entered the Theological College intending to be a preacher. Us oldies, and all the kids what had grown up with him, could see the sun shining on him.

"Well, come the time that Marvin was home from the Theological College on the long summer vacation. He was filled out, tall and big. He took the service at chapel on three Sundays, and he was good. I still remember him preaching on the life of Joseph, but never mind that. As I said he was good, and it was only afterwards that Emma said she and Rose didn't think he was as good as us men thought. Women, Mr Bonnar, can think and look deeper than men.

"Then comes the time he has to go back to college. Our Rose is a little poorly, and we think a spell in Perth would do her good. So it's planned for her to spend a month with her aunt up there, and as it's a long train journey everyone thinks it a good idea for her to travel up with Marvin. The train leaves at eight in the morning, and Luke is to take them to Timbertown.

"When they call to pick up Rose who's all ready, Luke says he's forgotten papers Jeff wants put into the bank, and he says he'll go back home on the timber truck what's due to pass on to the Inlet, get the papers and go on the truck to Timbertown, and so, after doing the business, come back home with the car.

"Off goes Rose with Marvin, luggage and all, all excited by the trip, looking her best in a blue dress and white hat and shoes. The driver of the truck and Luke found her on the track, on her hands and knees, groping about like she couldn't see, the blue dress in shreds. I wasn't handy when they brought her home. I didn't see her till after Emma had tended to her, and Emma said she looked like she'd been passed through a chaff-cutting machine.

"Looking over the years, me and Emma don't know if we made a mistake at that time. We should have rung the policeman to stop the raging tiger, but we didn't. We're isolated here. We keep our troubles to ourselves. At one time Mrs Stark had been a hospital nurse, and so Ted went down for her. Luke went after Marvin, but Marvin had driven on through Timbertown, and it wasn't till a fortnight later that the car was found at Kalgoorlie, left there by Marvin when he went through to the Eastern States."

Matt sighed his deep years-long anguish, was quiet for several minutes, and then asked the question he must have asked himself a thousand times:

"Why? Tell me why? Tell me how come an upstanding young feller should of done that? He's come of good stock. He's reared by God-fearing parents. He's loaded with gifts by the Almighty. And in a flash like, he turns from a human being into a bloody savage. You tell me how that can be."

Chapter Five

The Door

A cloud drifter over the karri and changed the deep blue of the sky to white, and the changing of the colour appeared to cause two kookaburras amid the branches to exchange low and sleepy chucklings. The usual rooster crowed and flapped his wings, and a dog came to the garden gate to peer in at the three sitting on the bench. When Matt spoke, he was calmer.

"Ted got the idea that Marvin arranged with Luke to forget the papers, and then take the milk truck back to get them, the truck being due at the time Rose left alone with Marvin. As I said, the truck came here from Timbertown, picked up Luke and went on down to Rhudder's homestead. There it took on the cream and what-ever, and left in half an hour for the return, calling in here for our cream cans.

"Seems that when Ted went down for Mrs Stark he had a word with Jeff, and it came out that the papers were supposed to be banked two days before. Ted said he thought Luke had forgotten them then, and made it the excuse for Marvin to travel alone with Rose that morning. They had a fight over it, did Ted and Luke, and a week later Luke went up to Perth and got himself a job there."

"And Rose? She recovered from her injuries, obviously," commented Bony.

"Yes, from her injuries but not from the other thing. Mrs Stark was mighty good to her, and so was Sarah, Jeff's wife. When we told Sarah what had happened she almost told us we were liars, but she had to believe it later on. It took Rose a long time to get past having nightmares, to get past crying fits long after the wounds she'd got healed up."

"But she recovered, didn't she?" pressed Bony. "She was courted and was married, and she had children and now is a happy woman, or I'm a duffer."

"That's so, Mr Bonnar," Emma agreed. "It was made up to her for all she suffered."

"Her husband doesn't know what happened to her?"

"No, no one does," replied Emma.

"Then how does Constable Sasoon and his wife know?"

"Because they've been our friends for years."

"Very well," Bony said, quickly. "Mr Jukes, you tell me what would be the result, other than being hanged, of you shooting Rhudder? No, I'll tell you. Your motive would be discovered and published to the world, and all the world, including your son-in-law would then know what did happen. I'm sure your daughter wouldn't want that."

"The world would never know the motive," Matt sullenly asserted.

"Yes, it would. The police or the prosecuting counsel would get it out of you. And besides, you continue to have warm regard for Jeff Rhudder, and how could you face him after shooting his son?"

"He's threatened to shoot him himself."

"Threatened, yes. Shoot him, I much doubt. Knock him down if physically able, yes. Order him from the house, yes. From what you tell me of this character, I feel sure he wouldn't go to the ultimate. And from what I am able to judge of your character, I am sure you wouldn't either. Had Marvin slain your Rose, it would have been quite different.

"And now, both of you," Bony continued in abruptly cheerful vein, "although you haven't consented to put me up, I shall thank you in advance. Please call me Nat, and I shall call you Matt and Emma. I have never failed to conclude an assignment, never failed to reach the murderer. I shall not fail this time. If I don't find Rhudder here, I shall catch up with him some other place. And then, for sure, he will be tried in Adelaide and hanged."

"That's what Sam said, Marvin having murdered in South Australia and not in New South Wales."

"With his record prior to the murder of the bookmaker, hanging will be inevitable, and your hunger for justice will be assuaged. Don't let it ride you any more, Matt. Think of those bonny grandchildren, and leave Marvin Rhudder to me and the judge. Look, is this your man, Karl Mueller, coming on the horse?"

"Good heavens!" exclaimed Emma, impulsively squeezing Bony's arm. "It must be twelve o'clock and no lunch ready."

"Remember I am Rose's friend," he reminded them. "As, in fact, I am."

Emma looked back at the visitor as she was about to pass into the house. She was smiling, for the weight of anxiety which had oppressed her since the return of Marvin Rhudder was lifted. Her husband continued moodily to look at the blaze of flowers in the strip of garden, and Bony watched the man and horse approaching from the cleared space beyond the mighty tree.

"Could you let me have a horse?" he asked.

"Any time. This afternoon? Karl'll bring one in."

"Not this afternoon. I am thinking you might like to show me the coast. Go fishing perhaps."

"All right. The tide will suit. We can fish it up. I'll check the gear." The stocky Jukes stood to say, before turning away: "I'm glad you came, Nat."

The dogs off the chain raced to meet the horseman. The kookaburras chortled, and a magpie swooped on the rooster and made him shout defiance and clap his wings. One Tree Farm was alive again.

Presently Karl Mueller came to sit with Bony, and with no more greeting than if they were fellow workers.

"Nice day."

Bony agreed, glancing at the weathered face and then into the friendly grey eyes. The wind ruffled Karl's blond hair streaked with grey at the temples.

"You travellin'?" asked Karl after the appropriate pause.

"No. I am visiting," Bony replied. "I'm staying a few weeks. Friend of Rose and her husband. I come from the Murchison."

"Friend of Rose, eh!" A slow smile spread over the rugged face. "Good! How's she? How's the littlies?"

Emma halted the lunch preparation to listen to Bony's answers, and smiled again when he made no mistake about names and age and sex, even the children's colouring. When she called them, Karl was warming to the visitor, and the conversation during the meal was almost gay.

Rhudder's Inlet was gradually revealed to Bony when Matt drove him in the utility over the undulating paddocks he farmed, where now and then the sheen of water appeared in the clefts of the changing horizon.

"Is it far off the road where Marvin crossed the creek and left his tracks?" Bony asked, and Matt said they could get the ute to within five hundred yards.

It was more than a creek. When in full flow in the rains it would be a turgid river a hundred yards wide here passing over flat country from the northern hills. After all the days since Marvin Rhudder splashed across its bordering flats, without troubling to remove his boots, some of the imprints on the caking mud were clear cut.

"Nothing much to see," remarked Matt as Bony stood and regarded the prints.

"I want only to memorize them," he was informed. "I see here where Sasoon took plaster casts, and his trackers did a good job concealing that operation. All right, Matt. We'll get on."

They topped a rise eventually and there lay Rhudder's Inlet displayed in all its beauty, and welcoming them with a drop in temperature of some ten or twelve degrees.

"Four miles long and two miles wide, or thereabouts," Matt said. "It's fed by three creeks like the one we just seen, and presently I'll show you it isn't an inlet at all."

The scent of algae met them, and when they were running beside the narrow strip of sand the gulls rose before the vehicle in indignant protest, and then settled again. Far ahead were the many buildings comprising the Rhudder homestead, and it appeared to lie hard against the tree-less, brown and dark-green sand-dunes, protecting it and the Inlet from the ocean beyond. Eastward were the open paddocks where cattle grazed, and in one, five hundred sheep. The fences were well maintained, and presently the buildings could be assessed. There was a garden, and, backed by a green hedge, several fruit trees. In contra-distinction to Matt's homestead, the place looked unprotected from the elements.

"Prosperous looking," commented Bony, and Matt said all the land was rich, adding:

"Jeff's grandfather settled here. Took up land both sides. Him and his wife and his sons slaved their guts out clearing and fencing with logs and brushwood, growing stuff to eat and living off the bandicoots and possums and the fish. There was always plenty of fish. There was never any money. They took produce on a bullock dray to Bunbury, nigh two hundred miles through the forests, and exchanged it for axes and saws and cloth to make clothes. Boots! They didn't want boots." Matt chuckled without mirth. "My old man came and took up our place, and slaved his guts out too, to get a start. In them days men was hardy."

The track skirted the garden-fence of posts and rails which probably had been erected a hundred years ago. Part of the house was built with tall six-feet-wide karri slabs, and part with modern machine timber, inset with modern windows, the whole now surmounted with corrugated iron painted red. On a wide and shadowed veranda appeared a man to wave to them, and Matt sounded his horn, saying:

"That's old Jeff. We might call in on the way home. Don't know how it is I call him old. Only one year older than me."

Now the track was merely a mark on the hard ground, and soon they were being pinched between the Inlet and the inner walls of great sand dunes, until they could proceed no farther. Carrying short rods, and tackle in a gunny-sack with sandwiches and a thermos, they passed to the extremity of the dunes and so emerged on to a wide wall of sea sand stretching across the entrance to the rising upland behind sheer cliffs bordered by clumps of tea-tree. Matt halted on the sand barrier to face the Inlet, and said:

"Used to be all clear here, and the river ran out through a deep cleft floored and walled with rock. Don't know what happened to make things different and old Jeff can't tell either. Anyway every so often the sea piles sand into this entrance like it is now, bottling back the river and creek water. Got to be a real big storm to do it. Time goes on and the water from the hills rises and rises to what you see it, and after more time another big storm will shift away all the sand and let the water out. I watched it happen once. Make a film you wouldn't forget."

The summit of the sand wall was something like ten feet above the Inlet surface, and perhaps fifty feet above the sea at low tide. It was a hundred yards thick and four hundred yards long, and required no imagination to picture what would happen when next the Inlet water was released.

The wind blew softly and almost coldly coming up from the far-away Antarctic. Crossing the sand bar they left its junction with the rising slope of earth and tea-tree, and went down to the narrow beach. This was steep and floored with shingle rocks the size of footballs, brown and grey and dark slate. The waves came in languidly, to rise abruptly into towering surf-free faces before leaning forward to smash down upon the giant shingle.

"Not much of a place to bathe," observed Bony. He stood watching for a few moments and then Matt saw him looking along the coast to the east. There were sand flats at the base of the dunes stretching for miles to terminate at a black headland. Off this section of coast stood rocks and rock-bars against which white water surged. There stood a large brownish rock and Bony asked what this was, as another farther on and farther seaward was grey.

"It's a mountain of seaweed," he was informed. "It's often about. The sea gathers the weed into a mound and then takes it away and builds it in another place. In my time I've never seen it anywhere but off the dunes. Never along these cliffs."

Bony turned in the indicated direction and was confronted by the picture of cliffs rising to four hundred feet, vast rocks isolated from the coast, great rock-bars extending into the ocean. It was an oddity how the dunes ended at the Inlet and the rock cliff-front began.

"The dunes wouldn't give a hiding-place to Marvin, but these cliffs certainly would," Bony said. "Let's have a look along there."

They trod water-logged sand, and climbed across rock-bars. They skirted vast towers of rock rising from the sandy areas. They crawled through rock tunnels where the sea swished and gurgled. They passed flat rock surfaces where there gaped great holes, Matt pointing out that to be knocked into one of them by a wave meant certain death. They came to a huge rock having seemingly sheer sides, and Matt said that there was only one way to the summit, and at the summit was a cave where a man could live in comfort.

Against the facets of the cliff-front were countless black patches denoting the entrance to caves, and these patches were at all heights above the ribbon of rock or sand beaches, now extended as the tide was out.

When Matt said that a large area of quiet water almost surrounded by a rock barrier was a good place to fish, Bony told him he wasn't interested in fishing at this moment, and they went on, to cross over a low headland, to pass shallow bays, and be attracted by a vast rock mountain which was presently seen to lie athwart a bay of glistening sand.

It was a spectacular monolith rising from the sea a thousand yards from the cliff. It stretched across the enclosed bay, stopping at both ends to admit a channel of water between itself and jutting rock-bars. The summit was comparatively level: the sides were sheer. The inner face presented to the cliff was also sheer, and between it and the edge of the sand, the channel appeared to be but fifty yards wide.

"Tide's about to turn," Matt said. "You'll see something when it does. We'd better take to this rock."

They climbed a rock at the cliff base, and while Bony was continuing to be awed by the vast rock slab as high as the cliff and all of half a mile wide. Matt spoke again.

"Marvin wrote a poem about that. Wasn't bad, either. He called it Australia's Front Door. To each side you can see the ships passing, and he said they were bound for one of Australia's Tradesmen's Entrances."

Chapter Six

The Fishermen

It was strange that, after thirteen years, and his heart heavy with rancour towards Marvin Rhudder for despoiling his daughter, Matthew Jukes should be unable to speak of him without evincing early admiration of the youth.

"Boy's talk," he went on. "Us two families were always proud of this place and that mighty rock out there. This coast belongs to us; every rock and stone and cliff and cave, the wind's never stale, and it's never hot like it can be inland. Either side that rock there's room enough, and the water is deep enough, to take a liner. On the inner side of it two liners could pass each other and not touch. At the east entrance there's a whirlpool what would sink a big ship. A door it is. Nothing afloat ever gets past that door: nothing afloat, no flotsam, no jetsam, nothing, ever comes ashore.

"Marvin put it right when he called it Australia's Front Door, shut for ever against the foreigners on ships what has to take 'em to Melbourne and Sydney, and other tradesmen's entrances. You might see a ship passing to left or right of the door, and looking no bigger than one of those gulls on top of it."

"Could we get closer to it across the sand?" Bony asked, himself caught up by the allegory.

"Too late, Nat. You'll see in a minute. With the change of the tide there's a sneaker what comes in with a rush. You'll see the water to the right side suddenly rise, and know it's coming. There's other places where you never know when a sneaker will come, and once it takes you you're finished. They said it was a sneaker what caught our Ted, but I think it must have been an earthquake-wave because Ted was too cunning to be caught. Pretty dangerous coast this. Which is why nobody comes here to fish. Now look!"

At first Bony could see no change in the water level at the west entrance past the Door. Then it did appear to rise relatively to the coastal rocks. He saw the wave sweeping in behind the Door, coming with astonishing speed to encircle it. It welled upward above the edge of the sand flat, rose many feet and rushed landward so high and so fast as to give him a spasm of fear although he was ten feet above the sand.

"If you was out there, it would knock you flat," Matt cried. "Ain't she a beaut?" The sneaker rushed upon their rock, swirled in foam about it, sped on to the cliff base where it seemed to tear at the barrier with futile, frantic rage. The pause preceded the retreat, the mad rush of water speeding back towards the channel behind the Door, and presently the sand flat was again bare. "Fall into that and you'd find yourself at the Door right close," Matt asserted quite unnecessarily. "I wanted you to see that. Just to prove you can't ever trust this sea. Looks innocent enough a day like this, but you take your eyes off it, and it'll get you sure enough."

"Must be terrific when it's real rough, Matt."

"Safer when it's blowing a gale. It's so nasty then that no one would take a chance with it. And don't you, ever."

Bony, curious about the ode to Australia's Front Door, asked what happened to it. This brought a chuckle from Matt.

"After he cleared out, the poem came back from a lit'ry magazine he sent it to. They said the poem was too imperialistic. You see, Marvin in the poem said the north of Australia was Australia's backside pointing at the Asians. Well, we'd better shift off this rock, with the tide coming in, or stay on it like a couple of shags till the tide goes out again. We'd better take some fish home. I know a place where we can get a ute load."

The wind was in the hair and in the dark eyes of this man who could hate for thirteen years, making of him at this moment a youth who would adventure go. They caught a dozen two-pound blackfish in fifteen minutes, and then climbed the cliff behind the Door. The way was steep but easy for active men. It was a test for the lungs, and the cigarette smoker breathed harder than the addict to the pipe when they reached the top.

Here, too, were the clumps of tea-tree bordering the cliff. Not to be confused with the ti-ti tree, the tea-tree clumps are similar to the Eskimo igloos if painted dark-green. The leaves are small and compact forming a close-knit covering erected by the twisting boughs. Often the clumps were separated, each being a hundred feet in circumference. Some overhung the cliff face; others were joined in larger masses among which an armed man could defy authority for weeks.

The place where Bony and Matt reached the top of the cliff was a confined grassy space, the grass tough and the ground hard. They sat on the cliff verge mainly to admire Australia's Front Door in its setting of blue ocean reaches either side, and the lazy surf caressing the black rocks as though lulling them into the belief that never again would there be a furious sea onslaught. The gulls were white patches on the summit of the mighty rock, and seals basking on a rocky headland beyond which Matt said was the whirlpool, were hard to distinguish until one 'flopped' into the water.

"What d'you think of this coast to hide away in?" Matt asked, and waved at the tea-tree skirting their picnic ground, and then pointing downward. "And the Police Heads in Bunbury thinking all Sasoon had to do was bring his offsiders and arrest Marvin."

Bony poured tea from the thermos into enamel cups before saying, with a shoulder shrug:

"It could never be done. That is other than with a Trojan Horse. The coast to the west looks to be even more rugged. A frontal attack on this Rhudder problem would certainly fail. Would you know all the caves and warrens in these Cliffs?"

"No." Matt was grim, but abruptly he smiled. "When old Jeff and me were kids we had to work long hours, and we didn't have much time to go exploring, or fishing. Not like the next generation what wasn't expected to do any work outside their schooling. Likely enough Marvin and the gang knew these cliffs and coast a thousand times better than Jeff or me. I'd say that if we searched the place yard by yard, Marvin could be watching from a cave we searched a couple of hours back. He was watching us all the time we were down below, I'll bet on that."

"Nevertheless, not being the hermit type he won't stay here for years," predicted Bony. "His kind must have the bright lights, and the darkness of ill-lit streets, and unwary victims. With him the stalking and the anticipation are more thrilling than the victory. He could have moved on already."

"He could have, Nat. More blame to me. I should of told Sasoon about him days before I did."

"You should have done so but you did not, and it's useless to look back. We accept the situation as it is and start from the present." Bony struck a match and lit the cigarette, and when Matt applied a match to his pipe there was no fighting with the wind. "One thing we may be sure about is that Marvin, if still here, is bound to visit his home for tucker and human contact, or someone at the homestead is bound to come out with supplies for him. And that is the link in Marvin's chain we have to find."

Matt nodded agreement, and Bony noted the smoke puffed from his mouth rising for several feet before the wind captured it. The explanation was simple. The breeze meeting the cliff-face continued upward beyond the cliff top before being driven inland and by this rotary action drawing inland air forward to the cliff edge. Where Matt was sitting with Bony the air was not quite still, and it brought the waxy scent of the tea-tree, and the scents of the tiny blue flowers sheltering in the tough and taller grass.

"You know of his record, I suppose?" Bony asked."

"Some of it. Perhaps enough of it to make me ashamed of being a man."

"Pity all men don't feel the same, Matt. His second crime in Sydney, or rather the second crime for which he was imprisoned, was stalking a couple in a Sydney park. Public park, you know. Lit with scattered lamps. Time, shortly after ten o'clock. They were an engaged couple, and were planning the house they would purchase. Friend Marvin bashed the man insensible and raped the girl. The stratum of morons in the community declared that the couple were in error in sitting in an illumined public park at ten o'clock on a hot night, and that by doing so they tempted overwhelmingly a mentally sick man.

"Marvin was sentenced to five years' gaol for rape. He was let out on a bond after three years."

"Why? You tell me that?" Matt said, fiercely. "Would he have got a longer term if they'd known about our Rose?"

"Probably a longer term, but doubtless he would have been released after serving three years. The psychiatrists all said he was suffering from a moral defect, not a character defect."

"Well, what's the difference?"

"Ask the psychiatrists. I don't know. Anyway, it was an excuse for the Parole Board to keep in favour with the Government, which likes to proclaim its merciful policy to criminals and thus hope for the votes of religious cranks and others. And the result of Marvin's second crime was that the man has been in a mental hospital ever since, and will surely remain there, and the girl walked over the Gap to her death a year later.

"To proceed with Marvin's career of bestial crime is nauseating. The highlights are those acts of bashing and rape for which he was given prison terms, and do not include those crimes for which he was strongly suspect, or when there wasn't sufficient evidence against him. During the space of thirteen years he was convicted five times and released on each occasion before the stupidly short sentence was served."

Bony lit another cigarette, and curiously watched the smoke being wafted to the cliff edge where it was caught in the uprush of air. He went on:

"We must render credit to Marvin where credit is due. From what you and others have told me of him before he went off the rails, he is a very clever man. He would stage his acts of piety at the correct moments. His behaviour in prison would be faultless. He would know the right answers to return to the psychiatrists, for when arrested in his room at one time he was found in possession of several standard works on psychology and psychiatry. And he must be given credit for choosing New South Wales in the era and place most favourable to his hunting instincts."

Bony stubbed the cigarette end against the heel of his shoe, and Matt saw him sniff as though suffering from sinus trouble.

"You and Jeff Rhudder aren't the only people who have threatened to shoot Marvin," Bony said, softly. "The same threat has been uttered in public by the father of the little girl who was attacked one night when returning home from buying a comic at the corner shop. I understand he was very keen, and perhaps he had some influence behind Marvin's decision to leave the safety of New South Wales for South Australia.

"I am telling you this because this Marvin Rhudder isn't the brave, the fearless leader, the intellectual, the good-looking boy and young man known to you up to the day he became Mr Hyde and ravished your daughter. There had to be a first. As a police investigator, I must obey the rules and the law, but as a private person and the father of three boys ..."

Bony suddenly went over backwards, gained his feet and raced out into the open behind the line of tea-tree. Astounded, yet Matt's reflexes were instant and he was almost beside him when Bony halted.

"What the hell!" he exclaimed, regarding Bony's flaring nostrils and wide, brilliant blue eyes. He felt Bony's restraining hand on his arm, and he stared in the direction of Bony's unwinking gaze. He knew Bony was concentrating beyond the nearest arboreal igloo, beyond it to the next, and then he noted a small area of movement on its painted covering.

"For a moment I saw only his back," Bony said, breathing hard. "I saw that he was armed with a rifle. He went into the tea-tree almost as though diving. Wait!" What Matt did not observe was the grass which had received the man's footprints, visibly rising to its original position. After so short a period it was hopeless to track. Concerned more with this minor problem than with the larger, Bony urged Matt to the cliff and out of sight of the man with the rifle.

"If he's in that bush why don't we get him?" Matt almost shouted. "He can't get away. He must be Marvin, the dirty swine."

"Calm down," ordered Bony. "We can't do any shooting with fishing-rods, and with the thermos for a bullet. Besides, I'm no hero."

"Nor me," agreed Matt, flexing his great hardened hands. "But we got to do something."

"We surely have, but what we have to do we do in our time, not his. What on earth would the Brass do if I suicided by walking against his rifle?"

"Nothing to be funny about, but I see your point."

"Good! We'll get along to the ute and then home. The sun's westering."

Matt slung the load of fish over a shoulder and Bony picked up the rods and thermos.

"When did it rain last?" he asked.

"Rain! We had two drops and a half a week ago. Haven't had a decent rain for five weeks."

Slowly, because Bony maintained attention on the ground, they proceeded between the tree-clumps or around the larger masses, sometimes able to skirt the sheer cliff drop. They came to an area where rabbits burrowed and, although the rodents hadn't fed on the grass, they had worn it away by their eternal skittering. Bony quartered it, halted, asking:

"None of the Rhudders has small feet, I take it. Here's a print made by a rubber-soled shoe size six. Could be made by the girl, Sadie. What would she be doing out here?"

"Collects sea-shells," informed Matt, and Bony countered him with:

"Hardly the place to find sea-shells, up on these cliffs."

"Easier travellin' up here than down below. Farther west, beyond Australia's Front Door, there's better hunting grounds for shell, and less dangerous, too. She's got a great collection, has Sadie. Writes pieces about 'em to the Perth papers, too." Bony broke into cheerful whistling, for he found prints of heavy male boots or shoes. "We call in on old Jeff?" suggested Matt.

"Not today," decided Bony. "Growing late and your Emma will be waiting for the fish, remember."

Chapter Seven

Nights Are for Blood-and-Gutzers

There was now no one on the veranda of the Inlet homestead, and the red and blue Holden standing outside the motor-shed belonged to Luke.

"Mark's got a flash red sports," Matt further mentioned. "And the Starks get about in a Vauxhall."

On the way to the coast Bony had been too interested in the plan of the homestead to take much notice of the rough but sturdy boat-shed opposite the front gate. He saw within it a boat, and Matt informed him it was a twelve-footer powered with an engine.

"Do you have one?" Bony asked, and Matt said, not since the children grew up.

All the gulls were afloat with the swans and the pelicans, and the ducks worked close inshore and took little notice of the utility. The wind had weakened and the sun was about to set, and Bony occupied these quiet moments to enlarge on his previously expressed warning.

"It's a pity you didn't obtain a clear picture of that man, Matt, but I believe we can be confident he was Marvin Rhudder, and we must proceed as though certain. Remember what I said about him, and also that Sasoon advised you to keep close to Emma. It was because I overheard you giving orders to Karl to repair a shed roof that I suggested our trip this afternoon."

"Marvin wouldn't have the gall to come to our place," asserted Matt, and Bony was impatient because in spite of the man's hatred of his daughter's ravisher, he did not even now, understand the menace.

"If subject to unfavourable circumstances, he might well do so," Bony persisted. "Marvin's a psychopath as well as a paranoiac. He's as dangerous as a tiger all the time, and a gorilla some of the time. He has what is necessary to think with, and in high degree, and thus he must be regarded as being always as dangerous as a gorilla and a tiger combined. That last woman he attacked in South Australia was sixty-eight. Age isn't important to him."

Following a prolonged silence, Matt said:

"D'you reckon he heard what we were talking about up on the cliff?"

"No. The back draught of air brought the smell of man to me, but it wasn't strong enough to indicate he was close enough to overhear. Now nothing of this to Emma or Karl."

The Inlet had been left behind and they were passing through a forest denuded of big trees, when Matt asked caustically:

"Aside from being a detective, you talk sense, Nat. What do we do if Marvin should appear at home?"

"Meet him with a gun, and, if you have to shoot, aim for his legs. Keep in mind always that to anticipate being hanged isn't conducive to mental relaxation. I keep in mind the poor lunatic in the asylum, the little girl, the other victims, and most especially, the possible victims-to-be."

Never doubting that her husband would return with fish, Emma had made the necessary preparation to include fish on the menu. She knew, too, that a two-pound blackfish nicely steamed and served with oyster sauce plus vegetables is enough for the average hungry man.

For Bony it had been both a varied and strenuous day, and when after dinner, the Jukes insisted he sit on the bench outside whilst the dinner chores were being done, he was more than ready to relax and meditate.

Where he sat he could hear the bustle and the conversation in the kitchen. In a yard calves bellowed for their mothers, and farther away pigs grunted or squeaked, and hens argued with whom they should roost. And now that the day was ended the karri tree was even more impressive as the lord of this world. Its trunk split the crimson western sky, and its mighty arms supported the celestial roof over the homestead. From far away, the restless ocean voiced its detestation of the grinning rocks.

Bony had achieved something this day. He had calmed the emotional tempest in Matthew Jukes. He had brought a measure of peace and thankfulness to the small woman who loved flowers and helpless things, and shrank from evil and violence. He had, during dinner, admitted his mission to the hired hand who was no hired hand in this household, and to Karl had given slight ease of mind. Now he was established, accepted, and their voices told him of what he had given.

Matt presently joined him, saying he had to lock up the poultry against the thieving foxes, and feed the calves with skimmed milk to keep them quiet for the night. His passage under the karri seemed to arouse the birds, because a magpie began softly to warble, and its song was taken up by several others. Butcher-birds in a tree robust but dwarfed by the karri joined in for a few moments. Emma and Karl came to sit with him and listen, too.

When the evening chorus was ended, Emma said faintly apologetic:

"We have an arrangement, Nat. Karl does the washing-up after dinner, and then for an hour I read aloud one of his books. It wouldn't disturb you, would it? You see, Matt likes to hear the readings as well."

"I should be disturbed if I were left out," protested Bony. "Then, when Matt comes in, we'll begin."

"What kind of books are yours, Karl?" Bony asked, and after waiting for help from Emma which perversely she didn't render, he said:

"Oh, all sorts, Nat. Blood-and-gutzers, you know. Can't afford real books with proper print and proper covers to 'em. You see, when I go across to Albany I calls in at a bookshop and buys up our stock for the year. This time I bought *Wuthering Heights* and a couple of Edgar Wallace's and a beaut looking job called *Ivanhoe*. The woman who runs the bookshop knows we don't go nap on the sexy stuff, and I got to rely on her what I bring home."

"I'm going to enjoy myself," decided Bony. "What is the book you're reading now, Emma?"

"*Ivanhoe*, it's a lovely tale."

"Better'n that *Wuthering Heights* one," Karl inserted. "Matt went off to sleep twice on that one, so we give it away for the *Green Archer*. Finished that a coupler nights back."

"You must get through a large number of books in a year, Karl."

"Too right. Least, Missus does. I can't read, having never gone to school. Then we changes 'em with people up at Timbertown, so we manages."

"Well now, don't let me delay the reading."

"Can't start without Matt, he'd go crook."

When Matt returned they sat at the table under the powerful pressure lamp suspended from the ceiling, and after them came the scent of flowers and the muted roaring of the Southern Ocean. Emma had gathered her spectacles and *Ivanhoe*, and opposite her sat Karl, his large face red and placid, his grey eyes holding the excitement of anticipation. In a corner was the radio, silent.

Emma began to read, and her clear enunciation at once pleased Bony. Then two events occurred to surprise him. A large black and white cat sprang up Karl's back and settled on a shoulder where it began to purr, and a little black dog laid its head on Bony's thigh and looked up at him, soulfully. Like the cat, the dog did not subsequently move.

Sitting at that end of the table opposite the door, he could see nothing beyond it, and realized how clear any one of them would be to a marksman outside. He found his mind wandering from the immortal story and was annoyed by the intruding pictures of a great rock slab, of hauling blackfish from the quiet hole before the tide returned, and of the igloo-shaped tea-tree and the man who had barely escaped being identified. Had Matt been able to do so, much would have been gained.

He was appalled but not dismayed by this southern coast, and the insuperable difficulties it presented in digging a man from it. There was another problem. The wire grass which had defeated him, after sighting the man who had tried to eavesdrop, wasn't universal, even along the cliff top. He had seen the prints on the rabbit-worn area, and, the ground inward from the cliff being less salted by the spindrift, bore good cattle-feed, was more open when the tea-tree gave place to shrubs and small scrub-trees. Among the larger scrub and trees of the back areas bordering the Inlet, tracking would be comparatively easy.

However, he was working under an assumed identity which he wished to maintain for several reasons. To be observed moving about looking for tracks would surely connect him with the wanted Marvin Rhudder, as well as making of himself a fine target for a sniper.

Although having expressed the doubt whether the man who vanished into a tea-tree clump was Marvin, in lieu of positive identification by Matt, Bony was strongly inclined to think it was; for if not, then what reason could another man, say Luke or Mark Rhudder, have for so acting? The scales weighed in favour of Marvin Rhudder being still in hiding on this coast. Favoured only, because the human tracks on the rabbit-scarred ground did not include the prints of Marvin Rhudder. Having studied prints made by the casts taken by Constable Sasoon, and having seen the line of prints on the mud beside the creek, he was sure of this. The cast prints gave him the man's foot size and other characteristics, and the mud prints in their relation each with the others gave additional characteristics, so that on crossing Rhudder's tracks elsewhere he wouldn't fail to recognize them.

He would have to proceed slowly and prod gently. He would have to evolve stratagems to conceal his purpose behind apparently normal activity as a visitor. He would have to wait patiently for one of several Mahomets to approach the Marvin Mountain.

Bony was thinking along these trails when Emma ceased the reading, closed the book and discarded the spectacles. The dog removed its head from Bony's thigh, and the cat rose and jumped from Karl's shoulder.

"Does the cat do that every night?" he asked Karl, and the hired hand smiled broadly before answering.

"Every night. They like listening, too."

"And in winter time when the door's shut they make a fuss to come in," added Emma. "We think it's the drone of my voice."

"No drone about that, Missus."

"Thank you, Karl. Shall we make a cup of tea? Or shall I ...?"

One of the dogs began barking and the small one inside raced out through the doorway. The cat walked on stiff legs to the doorway and stood there with its claws digging into the mat. Other dogs joined the first, and Matt said:

"Car coming up from the Inlet. Late, too."

Bony, unable to hear the sound of a car asked how Matt knew it, and Matt said by the manner in which the dogs barked. It was a full minute before Bony heard it.

"Wouldn't be going to Timbertown at this time of night," avowed Karl. "I'll see to that cup of tea, Missus."

When the car slowed to take the turn-off track, the dogs began to whine their welcome, and Matt rose to pass outside to meet the caller. Bony moved his chair away from the table, withdrawing from the brilliant circle of light. Then they heard Matt shouting to quieten the dogs, and a moment later there came to the silent three, a woman's voice.

"Well, I never!" exclaimed Emma. "It's Sadie Stark. I wonder what she wants this late?"

Footsteps sounded on the concrete approach, and the woman entered, followed by the polite Matt. Emma greeted her warmly, asking: "What's to do?" and Matt said: "Sadie's come for some of your patent cough balsam. Jeff's took sick and they've run out."

"Of course, dear," chirped Emma, beaming. "Sit down while I get a bottle. And meet Mr Nathaniel Bonnar. He won't mind you calling him Nat. Nat's a friend of Rose and her Harry."

Bony advanced into the light, taking his chair which he placed for the visitor. He was smiling in his easy fashion and saying it was nice to meet someone whom Rose had often mentioned, and the woman appeared to maintain her interest in Karl's blood-and-gutzer on the table, appeared to because although her face was angled to the book she was glancing upward at him. Faintly nodding, she said she was happy to meet any of Rose's friends, and sat on Bony's positioned chair. Bony retreated to obtain another for himself, and Matt gallantly breached a little silence.

"Sorry to hear old Jeff's sick again, Sadie. Oughta have that chest of his seen to. What with the sciatica he don't want nothing else."

"He won't call the doctor, Matt. You know how he is about it," she said, her voice slow, almost drawling.

Seated, her face remained inclined to the table edge, but her eyes, directed to Matt, moved to Bony. It was as though the strong light of the lamp was too much for them after the night trip.

"Are Rose and the children well?" she asked him, and when he said they were, and named each of the children, she smiled for the first time. The smile made her mouth a trifle large, and this might have been the effect of the angle at which she held her head. Her eyes were grey and large and steady, and her hands lay passive on her lap. Her attitude was one of deep meditation. Only her eyes failed to support the assumption.

Chapter Eight

A Varied Morning

At break of day the next morning Matt rode out and brought in the saddle horses, and, without waiting for breakfast, he and Bony rode to the ridge where Matt had maintained daily surveillance of the Rhudder homestead. At this point the entire Inlet with its major arms extending among the hills was clearly presented for inspection, and aided by the powerful binoculars, the homestead was brought close to the entranced Bony.

"Who will that be bringing the cows in for the milking?" Bony asked, handing the glasses to Matt.

"Sadie Stark. She often wears trousers, and does a fair amount of outside work. Sooner be out than do house-chores. I can see Mark in the yard at the milking shed."

Accepting the glasses, Bony again studied the rider behind the cows. Distance was too great to detect the girl's features, and being wiser, he could see it was a woman.

"How old is she?"

"Twenty-nine. Early seventeen when Marvin left."

"Has she always looked at people as though the light hurt her eyes?" pressed Bony, gazing at the wide sand-bar damming the Inlet water.

"Always had that trick. She'll look at you straight when she gets to know you." Matt paused for the next question and when it didn't come, said: "Me and Emma always liked Sadie. When she and the mother came to live with the Rhudders, Sadie was a tot, and was the youngest to play around with the Rhudder boys and our two kids. We thought one time our Ted and Sadie would marry, but nothing came of it."

"When was that?" was Bony's next question.

"Oh, about a year before Ted was took by the sea. I remember Emma getting curious about 'em and wanting to know, and Ted said he did ask Sadie and she put him off. Told him there was plenty of time, and she wanted to complete a book on shells. Something like that."

"She was collecting shells even then?"

"Oh yes. Been collecting for years. Took it up after Marvin cleared out."

The restless glasses halted at the sand-bar.

"If you lived at that homestead and wanted to take a walk along the cliffs, would you walk across the sand-bar or take the boat?"

"Take the boat. Shorter and quicker and less work than walking on the deep sand. Why?"

"Do the Rhudders own the land on the west side? Away over in the low timber that side, I can see what looks like the roof of a shed. What's there?"

"Small hut and mustering yards. Yes, they own the land, but soon after Luke went up to town for a job I rented it off 'em. There's ten square miles of good grazing in that block. On their side, the house side, they got something over fifty square miles of country. It's as much as Mark and Sadie can work together. Anyway, most of it is timber and grass behind the paddocks."

"There's a woman in the garden and a man crossing the yard to the motor-shed. Check, please."

Matt said the woman was Mrs Rhudder and the man her son Luke. The cows were in the milking-shed yard, and Matt who could, of course, see them without the glasses, said that the milk truck would arrive there at about eight-thirty that morning. Bony then switched back to the hut and yards and asked whether there were any cattle in the paddock they served.

"Too true," replied Matt. "Got to make the land pay the rent. There's sixty head in that paddock."

After gaining more information concerning distances and types of country, rivers and creeks and streams emptying in the Inlet from west and north, Bony was temporarily satisfied and suggested returning for breakfast. They went down the steep inner slope from the ridge to the tethered horses, and arrived home at seven. Following a leisurely breakfast, Bony operated his line of communication with Senior Constable Sasoon.

"Sam, what are you doing tonight?" he asked.

"Whatever you have in mind, is what I'm doing tonight."

Bony turned to capture Emma's attention before continuing.

"We caught some nice blackfish yesterday, and I thought the wife and you would like to have some. Otherwise according to Emma, we are going to eat fish until we look like fish. What of the suggestion of coming down this evening with your wife? I'm sure Emma is dying for a gossip about this, that, and the rest."

"Be there about eight. Suit?"

"I think so. The fish will keep. They're on the ice."

Replacing the receiver, Bony turned back to the smiling Emma, saying diffidently:

"I have to talk with Sasoon, and we can get more fish, can't we?"

"Of course. And I'd like a gossip with Else. Anyway we can co-operate, just tell us, Nat."

"Splendid! What are you doing this morning?"

"Just the chores. And no one told you to make your own bed."

"Ah, but I shall help you that you shall help me. Those breakfast things I am going to wash and rinse and dry. You shall do the other chores, and then we'll both be free."

Emma laughed outright, and wanted to know what freedom.

"Well, I shall be free to sit here and drink tea and smoke cigarettes and ask questions, and you will be free to drink tea and answer the questions. We won't be interrupted, as Matt is working with Karl. How does that appeal to you?"

"It should be interesting. But I wash up."

"I'm sure you would not like to see my most severe expression."

Fifteen minutes later when she saw the low piles of washed crockery, and found Bony spooning tea into the pot, she said gaily:

"There's the proof you've been well trained."

"I'm the tamest lion you've ever had in your house. Have you done your jobs yet?"

"Not quite."

"Have you a family album?" Emma nodded. "I could look at that while you're finishing your work."

He watched her open a drawer of a roll-top desk, saw her remove tissue paper from about a handsome leather-covered photo album, and this she brought to the table to place it with care amounting to reverence. She said, her eyes no longer joyous:

"It's a record of our Ted, according to the years. All the others are in it, too."

"Then I'll wait until we can look at it together. It sounds like someone coming, anyway."

The dogs began to bark, and Emma nodded and returned the album to the drawer. At the doorway Bony could hear the car in the distance, and knew it was coming from the Inlet. He sought the gunny-sack containing the fishing gear, and sat on the outside bench fiddling with line and hooks. A few moments later the chained dogs whined their greeting, and the car turned in off the road and was stopped in the shadow of the great trunk of the karri tree.

The man who left the driving wheel and came walking to the garden gate was both wide and thick. He rolled slightly like a sailor long at sea, a powerful man close to six feet tall. Hatless, his brown hair was overly long, and on reaching the gate there was a slight smile lighting the heavy face and the small brown eyes. Emma came to the door to welcome him.

"Why, Luke! Are you off to town?"

He came in through the small garden before replying that he was and asking did she want anything brought back. Emma then introduced Bony to him.

"Nat Bonnar! Glad to meet you. Sadie said she met you last night. Oh holiday, eh! Good place for a spell, though I say it myself."

They shook hands and his clasp wasn't weak.

"Luke lives in Perth," Emma explained. "You'll find it hotter up there, Luke."

"Clammy, Emma, clammy. Not like home where's it's always cool. You'd find the difference from the Murchison, Nat. It is the Murchison? Or is Sadie wrong on that point?"

"Murchison, all right. Seventy miles east of Mount Magnet."

"Phew! Red hot and full of dust this time of year. Staying down long?"

"Three weeks, unless something goes wrong. Hope not, because I think I shall like it here very much. Good fishing, anyway."

"Well, I'd better push on. If you think of anything you want, Emma, ring the store. I've got to go there. And if I don't see you on my way back, Nat, how about running down for a chat. The old dad would like to natter. Bit of an invalid, you know. He asked me to invite you."

"I shall be delighted, Luke."

"Well, make it soon. Tomorrow, if you care to. I'll be home then to show you around. Have to go back to the grind on Friday. Cheers!"

They watched him enter his car, a powerful man in the prime of life, a thrusting man who might go far in a city like Perth. Bony tried to see in his broad back and his height the glimpse of the figure disappearing into the tea-tree clump, and failed. He waved and Emma waved back, and then when on the road he sounded his horn derisively.

Emma went in and Bony sauntered to the gate and then about the open space, seemingly casual in his examination of Luke Rhudder's shoe-prints. There was general similarity with those made by Marvin, more especially in the length of stride and the depth of each heel at the extremity. If he had not just seen the man these tracks would tell of youthful vigour and excellent health. The same tracks were on the rabbit warren on the cliff.

"What are you looking for? Lost something?" Emma asked before he noticed her coming.

"I am always looking for something," he told her. "Would Matt have any plaster of Paris, by any chance?"

"Some in a tin in the shed, I think, Nat. Matt had it to repair a ceiling last month. Shall I get it?"

"Please. I'll go with you. I'll want a mixing board and water, too."

Later she watched him carefully pour the mixture into a selected print, and gently smooth the top surface. He brought a wood case which he placed over the cast to shield until dry. Then:

"That tea I made is going to be well stewed," he said. "We'd better go in and see what's happened to it."

After tea and biscuits, Emma again brought the album to the table and was invited to be seated with Bony. She watched covertly this stranger to her home, noting his straight black hair meticulously groomed, observing the line of forehead and cheek and chin, the long dark ringers caressing the leaves of her precious album. She had noted a moment before how carefully he had stubbed his cigarette to prevent ash possibly falling upon it.

Turning over the pages, history was presented in the appearance first of one baby and then another, and their growing up to small and sturdy children. Bony was informed they were Ted and Rose. Ted was dark and his sister fair. Then there were pictures of two gangling girls, the brown haired one taller than Rose and more angular, and named Sadie Stark.

Three boys entered the record. Two were stocky and giving certitude of the men they were to become, one was thin and looked frail compared with the others. Pictures of the five children were plentiful, and they grew beneath Bony's page-turning fingers until growth stopped and for long moments Bony studied one group caught on a house veranda. The two girls were now in school uniform. Seated together, Rose Jukes was obviously a pretty girl inclined to plumpness, and Sadie Stark still needed to fill out.

Behind them stood the three boys, Marvin, Luke and Mark. Mark was dark, and still thin, but as tall as Marvin who was taller than Luke by an inch or two. Superficially they were just a parcel of ordinary out-of-doors country children in their best clothes. Ted Jukes was missing, and Emma explained that Ted took the picture and would be in the next one taken by Marvin.

Although Bony wasn't interested in Ted Jukes he pretended to be for Emma's sake, and then went back to the first where Marvin stood with his brothers. Emma said in answer that Marvin would be fifteen years old, and, moving on, every picture of him betrayed the exhibitionist. His hair was carefully combed with the Napoleon quiff pasted into position, and in several ways he looked not unlike the Emperor from the eyebrows upward. He appeared with a flower in his coat lapel; with a book elegantly poised, with a writing-pad on the top of crossed legs, and an expression of intellectual concentration.

In the following pictures where Ted Jukes, who had his mother's colouring and features, appeared with Marvin Rhudder, Bony noted it was the latter who attained predominance of place and attitude, and that in those pictures minus Marvin, Emma's son was more at ease, more sure of himself.

Emma, still shyly watching this man who had entered their lives, witnessed the expression on his dark face change to one of puzzlement. She was aware he saw nothing of what lay beyond the oblong of the rear door, that what he was seeing none would ever know. Slowly his lean fingers closed the album, and the long hands lifted it and placed it down farther from him, and somehow she knew it was done merely to avoid pushing it away when finished with, like one of Karl's blood-and-gutzers. He said:

"Thank you, Emma, for permitting me to share something dear to you. Now please answer me one more question, knowing the answer comes from your heart. It is this: Were you Marvin's mother, would you help, sustain, protect him, still love him?"

Emma pondered for a moment. Then she crossed to the desk with the album. She stood awhile gazing down at it before closing the drawer. When she turned about the movement was swift, but her voice was low.

"Yes."

Chapter Nine

A Hut With a History

Matt came in before lunch and Bony called for the Land Department's maps of the area. These they studied together, and the result was a picture of the subdivisions of both the Rhudder and Jukes properties marked by the fences, old bush tracks and gates and waters.

On the table with the maps was the plaster cast of Luke's footprint, and when Emma suggested she would like to lay the cloth, Bony took the cast to his room, and the plans were put away. Matt opened a bottle of beer, and for several minutes Bony stood just outside the door, sipping from the glass and examining a problem. He recalled Sasoon's report on the official visit to the Rhudder homestead, when Jeff Rhudder slightly stressed the verb in its past tense ... "What *did* you come down for?" Why, indeed, had Luke come from Perth a day or so after Marvin arrived home, if not in connexion with that arrival? He was now to return to Perth on the coming Friday. What had happened, or what had been accomplished, relative to the purpose of his visit?

Before Luke called on his way to Timbertown, Bony had planned to place observers on the ridge overlooking the Inlet. It was his reason for inviting Sasoon down this coming evening, but the plan now would have to be put into operation as soon as possible.

At Timbertown there was, fortunately, an automatic exchange, and he rang through to Sasoon.

"I want two trackers down here to camp for several days. Could you spare your Constable Breckoff for a day or two to establish the camp and certain routine?"

"Right away, Nat," Sasoon replied without hesitation.

"But not in daylight. No one at your end must know of the engagement of the trackers or the reason. Clear?"

"Yes, that's plain. Can do."

"Good! See you both as fixed this morning. About eight. Luke in town?" Sasoon said Luke had been there for a couple of hours. "Before you leave call on the postmaster as we arranged."

At lunch, Bony asked Matt when the yards and adjacent hut had last been used, and Matt said it was three months ago, and he was thinking of mustering cattle there for marketable beasts. This pleased Bony greatly, for there would be no fresh horse-tracks to confuse, and no human prints about the hut. Could he have a horse this afternoon? Of course he could. He rode away immediately after lunch, leaving Matt wondering, and Emma quietly expectant.

The horse was black, strong, a knowledgeable stock horse, free in action and having a tendency to be stubborn until Bony discussed with him the necessity of co-operation. The day was beyond reproach, a faint wind bringing the music of the surf to the hills and the song of the bees among the wild flowers in the dells.

The man dressed in brown shirt and slacks, black hair wild in the breeze looked good, too. Astride this mettlesome gelding, there was nothing in his seat of the cavalryman or mounted police trooper, and nothing of the animal of training and discipline. Both were as free of inhibitions as Bellerophon on the back of Pegasus.

They followed what was little better than a trail, probably opened when Matt first took up the Rhudder land west of the Inlet, for on it were the indentations of truck wheels and cattle hooves, and the 'road' lay across hillsides massed with scrub, and dells where grew the cedar woods and the jarrahs and mighty karri. It lay across the fern floors of wider valleys, spongy and giving forth the aroma of Time beyond the conception of Man. They passed by gatherings of paper-bark trees, all twisted and grey and as old as Methuselah. And they came to a wire-gate in the wire-fence crossing the northern boundary of the Rhudder land.

Soon thereafter the country became more open with wide areas of good grass, and Bony urged the horse onward with shouts and bush song, and the animal laid his ears back and thoroughly enjoyed the spasm of wildness in his rider. Gradually the noise of the sea increased, and gradually the timber changed to gum saplings, with beyond them to the left the sheen of water. Bony rode from the track and headed down the slope through the saplings and to the long grassy slope ending at the west shore of Rhudder's Inlet.

Ah! Hope fulfilled! There were cattle feeding or lying down along this western slope. Far to the south the sun glinted on the windows of the homestead, and a little to the right the white sand-bar imprisoned the water. Without doubt those at the homestead would see the stranger from the Murchison District 'pushing' cattle up and from the slope as part of another of Matt's cattle musters. This Bony proceeded to do with pistol-cracking stock-whip, and occasional shout. When opposite the homestead, the west wind would surely carry the sounds across the water. He was a northern stockman assisting his host with a chore.

However, the chore did not prevent him from doing a little work for the State.

Riding along the slope, turning the cattle up and into the timber and scrub, he maintained vigilant attention to the shore, and thus, eventually coming opposite the house found where the Rhudder boat had been beached, having on three occasions been drawn up to the dry sand. Sure that he was being watched, he did not pause for a moment, riding on to the junction of the sand-bar with the slope and then up the slope to skirt the inner edges of the tea-tree.

Whilst still in view of those at the homestead, he turned away from the cliff into the sparse scrub and better grassland, as though intending to return at the rear of the disturbed cattle and again urge them towards the cattle yards. It was when out of sight, that he swung about to gallop to the cliff edge behind Australia's Front Door.

So clear was the day that it appeared possible to toss a stone to the top of it. The tide was ebbing but the sand-flat between it and the cliff base was still covered. The water looked motionless and in places where the wind was defeated by rocks he could see from his elevation the sand-ripples.

Reining back his horse he rode westward outside the teatree, the animal content to walk at a smart pace. In little less than half a mile he had to cross a wide but shallow watergutter, and here looked for tracks and did see the imprints of sand-shoes of small size which must have been worn by Sadie Stark.

Matt was right when he said that the coast farther west was superior for shell hunting, for the iron front of the cliffs was less steep, much more indented, and rose above miniature coves and inlets. Farther on the land was higher, the cliffs again precipitous and unguarded by rock out-thrusts. In a small cove Bony found Sadie Stark with her collecting basket, a tiny figure in dark blue and grey slacks, and wearing sand-shoes.

Riding towards the hut and yards, Bony recalled the boat marks. Today, at any rate, Sadie hadn't crossed in the boat, but by the sand-bar. He conjured the picture of her, stooping over the gravel patches, a tiny lone figure on all this tremendous coast.

The stockyards, built with heavy rails and uprights, and the small slab hut with its paperbark roof, were situated outside a ring of paperbark trees, all grey-white of trunk and branch. Inside the ring was a flat expanse which in wet weather would be a shallow lagoon.

Having neck-roped the horse to a tree, Bony felt the bark to be dry and yielding. He was able to tear off a strip, to find it composed of layer above layer of paper-thin wafers which could be parted without trouble. Under the outer one the wafers were flesh-coloured, and he estimated that fifty of them made the thickness of the bark he had torn away, and there were wafers under that. Should each layer represent a year's growth these trees must be hundreds of years old.

Other matters were much more important, and, discarding the bark, he circled the yards to find, as Matt had said, that they hadn't been used for months.

Leaning against a massive gate-post, he studied the situation of the hut whilst rolling and smoking a cigarette. The hut was a hundred-odd yards outside the paperbarks. It was obviously of one room only, having a chimney and one door, and no window. The ground about it, as elsewhere, had been churned to dust by cattle hooves, and rain had hardened the thin crust, and the wind had eventually removed the crust and driven the dust against tree-falls and cattle droppings. It required little effort to scoop a hole with the heel of his boot and bury the cigarette butt.

As it was normal for anyone coming to this place to want to look inside the old hut, he strode to it without bothering about his tracks. Before opening the door, he went round the back, to find there a well. He found, too, that the ground surface about the hut was not as that over which he had crossed from the yards and his interest was quickened by what to him was obvious. A previous visitor had carefully wiped out his tracks by smoothing the surface with a leafy tree-sucker. When it was done was impossible to estimate, for the wind had blotted out the minute ripples produced by the sweeping leaves.

Opening the door wide, he stood looking into the interior. The floor was of white-ant nest, first laid as rubble, then watered and pounded flat to dry like cement. Opposite the door was a rough table hinged to the wall and supported with corner props. Above it was a shelf, and on this were several large tins originally containing biscuits. Beside the table was a wood case which at one time contained two four-gallon tins of petrol or oil, and plainly used as a seat.

Stepping inside he found no disorder, and his first interest was in the open hearth. Fine wood ash there was, inches deep.

There was a short-handled shovel in a corner and Bony dug among the ash, disclosing nothing unusual. Looking up the chimney he could see the sky but no spider webs, which after three months could be expected. He returned to the table. Under it and where it joined the wall there were no webs nor were there any in and about the case. The beams supporting the roof were festooned with web, as were the corners.

The place had been occupied quite recently.

Bony closed the door and sat on the case in the almost complete darkness, and now he closed his eyes the better to concentrate on what his nose might detect. Sniffing with intent, he decided that the air wasn't as stale as three months would have made it. There was the smell of eucalyptus oil mixed with ... Of course, it was wood smoke clinging to the walls and the roof, and incorporated with it was the smell of grilling meat. He remembered seeing the wire griller hanging from a wall nail, found it in the dark, and by touch knew it had been used within the last month.

His nose registered another smell, and he was tiring of the effort to establish it when he named it. The smell of a human being, and not an unwashed human being, either. It contained a soapy component, and presently Bony thought it likely to be of shaving soap. There was yet another, the third scent which was not more prominent than the others in this general mixture.

After several minutes of trying to track down this third scent he surrendered on the principle of pushing a thing out of the mind when the mind itself will claim it.

Three months since anyone had been here, according to Matt's knowledge. Well, the origins of these three scents were certainly less than three months old. Although it seemed unlikely, it could be that Marvin had stayed at this hut, unlikely because he would be unaware when Matt would again muster stock, or ride to inspect the yards.

Having fastened the door, Bony proceeded on his routine investigation of the surrounding country, making first a small circle, then a larger and so on, and found that cutting each circle towards the Inlet was the evidential mark of the leafy sucker. Now he walked towards the Inlet, zigzagging to and fro across the imagined straight line until the scrub trees ahead began to admit the open space of the Inlet. He was obliged to step across a wide water gutter where the sand had been left rippled by the last run of water. Here he paused to examine the gutter in both directions, and smiled grimly when he found a small area of sand that had been smoothed to obliterate a footprint. From within fifty yards of the hut to this place, a man could walk from grass tussock to tussock and not leave a print, and the grass tussocks continued on the far side towards the Inlet.

He who had been so careful to obliterate his prints, and avoid leaving so many others, had been making for the Inlet where the boat had left its marks, and it would not be possible to proceed five hundred yards beyond an ancient, lightning blasted red gum-tree without being seen from the homestead.

It isn't in the nature of the aborigine to give up until forced by circumstances, and Bony, being allied with them, continued on to the gum-tree. The lightning bolt had spared one branch to cast a deep shade, and about the tree, cattle had camped and churned the ground as that about the yards and hut. Close to the butt of the tree, the leafy sucker had again been used to smooth out a track.

The ground had not been so treated beyond the tree, and it was obvious that the person he had been tracking had come only so far and not on to the Inlet. The tree became significant.

From various quarters, Bony studied it from the butt upward to the shattered crown a few feet above the remaining branch. The study resulted in observing a broken sucker which had sprouted from the trunk at the place where it could be easily climbed.

Climb a tree! Adults don't climb trees unless for birds' eggs. Now an adult did climb this one to discover the purpose of the previous climber. Bony found it not at all difficult, and soon he came to the junction of the living branch and then on and up to the blasted top which he found jagged-edged and hollowed by the fire resulting from the strike.

Down to the junction of the branch the trunk was merely a fire-hollowed shell having a diameter of something like five feet. Bony peered down into the gloom, and could see an object which could well be a box with metal fittings.

Chapter Ten

Bony's Surprise

The great karri tree split the glowing sunset sky like an iron wedge when all the dogs broke into frenzied barking so unlike their greeting of a car coming up from the Inlet. A magpie skittered from the arboreal roof above the house, and somewhere a kookaburra ha-ha-ha'd as though finding humour in the magpie's antics.

Emma had prepared an early dinner this evening, and now Karl came in from locking up the hens and tending to the hungry calves. Matt and Emma went out to welcome Senior Constable Sasoon and his Elsie. Karl shouted at the dogs and their uproar was replaced by the voices of the women raised by the meeting of two friends of long standing. The scene wasn't unusual, made even commonplace when the policeman removed from his car a carton of beer.

"Evening, Nat!" he said almost casually to Bony. "How's things?"

"I hope, excellent," gravely replied Bony.

"Been a good day, eh?"

"Wonderful. Perfect weather."

"Didn't notice, much. Been busy all afternoon. Dry as dust." Proving he was on special terms with the Jukes, Sasoon brought up two bottles of beer, winked at Karl to fetch an opener, and himself brought glasses from the dresser. "Breckoff will be here about eleven."

"He was able to collect the trackers?" Bony asked.

"Yes. Only one young one, though. Old Lew is the other. Lew can't jump high these days, but he's a wise old coot. You got work for 'em?"

"Work!" echoed Bony, smiling. "They're in for a real holiday."

"Lucky swabs. Wish I was. Well, here's how."

They sat, Australian fashion, at the table, the men in open-neck shirts and sleeves rolled high. The two women went off on their own affairs, and Karl was invited by Bony to sit in with the party.

"I have appointed Karl the timekeeper," Bony stated. "What time did Luke pass on his way home, Karl?"

"Twenty past five," replied the member of the Jukes family. "Didn't come in."

Sasoon laid a typed report before Bony, saying:

"When in town today, he went to the post office twice, the first to dispatch two telegrams and make a phone call to Perth, the second time to collect two telegrams. He went into a store where he bought tobacco and two expensive boxes of chocolates. He spent a couple of hours this morning with two men in the hotel, and again visited the hotel with a man who's a stranger to us."

Taking up the paper, Bony read:

1. 10.12 this a.m. Reply-paid telegram to Postmaster at Mount Magnet. Message: Am expecting important telegram from Sydney. Please let me know immediately if same received, and post it on to me.
Signed: Nathaniel Bonnar, Post Office, Timbertown.

1. OK 10.12 this a.m. Reply-paid telegram to Mrs Rose Curnow, 13 Tent Street, Geraldton. Message: Having wonderful time. Please inform immediately if you able to spend week with children at my place shortly before Easter.
Signed: Nat Bonnar, Post Office, Timbertown.

2. 10.20 this a.m. Telephoned Mrs Luke Rhudder, trunk line, Perth, asking after health of family and saying would be home Friday late.

3. 3.50 this p.m. Collected two telegrams. 1. From Post Master, Mount Magnet. Message: Telegram not yet received. Leave a fish in the sea for me. Charlie. 2. From Mrs Rose Curnow, Geraldton. Delighted to accept. You name the date sometime. Give love to Dad and Mum. Rose.

Bony looked up from the report into Sasoon's quizzing grey eyes, and passed it on to Matt. Waiting for Matt to comment, he rolled a cigarette and applied a light before saying:

"Messages designed to test my background, obviously. It's as well that I took pains to create it, isn't it?"

Matt required explanation, and was told that Bony now being Nat Bonnar down from the north on holiday, and the friend of his daughter and her husband, had had to take steps to forestall just such a test as this made by Luke Rhudder.

"Luke's telegrams prove that Marvin is down there somewhere, or was down there somewhere, and therefore the identity of any stranger must be checked," Bony continued. "Had the recipients of the telegrams replied asking who the heck Bonnar was then the Nat Bonnar with you must be a police investigator. Naturally, we don't want them to think such evil of me."

"You just said Marvin is down there or was down there," Sasoon queried. "Are you thinking he's not there now?"

"I have thought all along that he might have left before I came. The fact that Luke intends to return to Perth on Friday might mean that Marvin has cleared out, and he, Luke, is no longer needed at home. We must, of course, proceed on the presumption that he is still around."

"What about that bloke in the tea-tree?" questioned Matt, his dark eyes intense.

"I grant that the odds favour Marvin."

"Bloke in the tea-tree, eh! So I don't know everything."

"Matt and I have our little adventures, Sam. That coast is crammed full with adventures. You tell of ours, Matt."

Matt gave the bare facts.

"You can't be sure?" pressed the policeman.

"No, I only seen a flash of him more than half-way into the scrub," replied Matt. "And remember, I haven't seen Marvin for thirteen years."

"Was it Luke, d'you reckon? Him and Marvin is the same build. What d'you think, Karl? You saw him on the way home."

"Could have been," responded Karl. "Marvin ain't lost none of his size. He was taller than Luke, but just as wide. I'll tell you summat. From how Matt tells it the feller was pretty nippy on his feet. Now Luke's been livin' soft in a city job for years, and Marvin's lived hard and even got a job on a cattle boat where they got to work and be nippy on their feet. I'm gamblin' on ..."

Karl was stopped by the shrilling of the telephone. Sasoon automatically began to rise to take the call, remembered where he was and relaxed, looking at Bony.

"You take it, Matt. Everyone else quiet, please."

Matt crossed to the instrument and when he spoke they knew who was calling.

"That you, Jeff? How you doing? Cough better? Good! Yes, I think so. Yes, why not? I'll ask him." Matt waved the instrument from his mouth, and to Bony said: "Mr Rhudder. Wants me and Emma and you to run down tomorrow for a gossip and afternoon tea. Suit you?"

"Yes, and tell Mr Rhudder I appreciate the invitation."

This subject ended, Matt and Jeff talked about cattle prices, and Bony printed on the back of Sasoon's report the words:

"If Jeff mentions a muster, tell him you and I were out in the paddock this afternoon."

This he took to Matt, holding it for him to read until Matt nodded. Sure enough the prompting was needed, for Matt said into the instrument: "Too right, Jeff. Me and Nat rode out this afternoon to see what was good enough to market. Might send in a dozen fats. Prices are high, especially for vealers. Goodoh! See you all tomorrow."

Matt returned to his chair, looked at Bony, then at Sasoon for comment. Neither gave it. The two women came into the room, and Emma wanted to know who rang. Seeing their serious expression, she said:

"Oh, if it's police business ..."

"Nothing of the kind, Emma," Bony told her. "It was quite pleasant, actually. You and Matt and I have been invited out to afternoon tea."

"Truly? What a thrill. I suppose with the minister and his wife?"

"No, nothing so exciting. The invitation came from Jeff."

"Old Jeff! But we haven't been down there for a year."

"We are going there tomorrow, anyhow," her husband confirmed.

"Well, I never! And look, Else, they've drunk all the beer."

"Not yet," Sam told her. "I don't agree with women guzzling beer, so I brought a bottle of sherry. I'll get it from the car."

"The man who never forgets," exclaimed Elsie.

"No, and now we'll have supper. Come on, Else, we'll get it."

Elsie was laying the cloth and Emma was returning with a dish of sandwiches when Sam returned with the wine and bottles of lemonade. The supper, already prepared, was swiftly on the table, and Bony then said:

"After supper I've a little surprise for all of us."

"Oh, indeed, Nat. What is it?" exclaimed Emma.

"The very twin of Pandora's Box. You and Elsie shall toss for who opens it."

"I can't wait," pleaded the policeman's wife.

"You will," her husband said, his mind still on the call from the Inlet. "Looks like you passed their test, Nat. Looks like Marvin isn't hid-up at the homestead, doesn't it?"

"The purpose could be to test me further, Sam. Jeff and his sons know much about cattle and sheep. I am supposed to manage a station." Bony smiled. "I never set a background without proof to support it, give it reality. The visit will be interesting."

Emma's tasty supper was something to behold. The table was loaded with sandwiches and sponge cakes and buttered scones and cake and savouries enough for twenty guests. Sam's bottles heightened the effect. But after the table was cleared and the coffee set before them, Bony was not left to appreciate it.

"Where's that box?" Emma demanded.

"Yes, where? Produce Pandora's Box," ordered Elsie.

"Who's going to open it?" Karl interposed, his wide face and grey eyes reflecting their excitement as though all were children at a Christmas party. And Bony looking from one to another was glad that there are unsophisticated people in this world, and desperately hoped that the box would disappoint neither them nor himself.

Elsie having won the toss, he said he would fetch the box. They heard the garden gate-latch click and looked at each other amused and expectant, even Sasoon in this party-spirit temporarily forgetful of the real business of the evening. When Bony returned the women uttered faint cries of disappointment.

Bony carried a suitcase by the handle, and Sasoon noticed how careful he was to place the case on the table without the assistance of his other hand. It was of medium size, good quality and brown of colour.

"A table knife, Karl," he said, and when the knife was brought he stepped back and beamed upon the company. "I don't know what is in this Pandora's Box. You will recall that in the very ancient days the chief god was a fellow called Zeus, and like all modern dictators he was a paranoiac. Someone annoyed him and so he withdrew the blessing of fire from men. A fellow god, named Prometheus, tricked Zeus by making a torch and lighting it at the Sun, then taking the torch down to Earth. This annoyed the Dictator still more, and so he made a very beautiful woman and sent her down to Earth with a wonderful box in her arms. All the boys crowded around her, as they do even to this day, and when she opened the box all the terrible afflictions mankind has since suffered escaped, leaving behind only Hope. Thus with the coming of the First Woman universal misery was introduced among men."

"How awful," exclaimed Emma, and Elsie giggled.

"Nothing to laugh at," Sasoon sternly told his wife. "Go on, Nat. What's the catch? I'll buy it."

"I found this box in a dark pit at the end of a long and dangerous journey," continued Bony. "I have taken all care possible with it to preserve as much as possible—fingerprints. So, no one is to touch it. I will open the side fasteners with the point of this knife. Good! Now I'll use the knife to push to one side the lock, thus." The lid of the case jerked slightly upward, and Bony presented the knife to Elsie. "Now, with the knife point raise the lid so that it will remain open."

Sasoon's wife accepted the knife, gazing wonderingly at Bony. The others, save Karl, were still and silent. Karl's breathing rasped through his nose, and his eyes were big. The large woman placed the end of the knife under the edge of the lid and raised it. Then she tittered.

"Take the shirts and put them to one side without touching the case," Bony requested, and Elsie removed four washed and ironed shirts. "Now those ties. Thank you. Now shoes. They are soiled aren't they? The sports jacket and trousers. Now the book. Thank you. Ah, *The Plays of Oscar Wilde.* The shaving kit. Now what! Leave that large and bulky envelope, please."

The envelope measured about eighteen inches by twelve. The flap was unstuck, and with the knife, Bony lifted the envelope by that end, rested it against the edge of the case and raised the flap, then widened the opening with the tip of his other finger.

"Blimey!" gasped Sasoon. "Oh, Emma, look!" Elsie exclaimed.

Inside the envelope, banded and wadded, were masses of Australian currency.

Chapter Eleven

The Tea Party

Bony departed the next morning at sun-up with Breckoff and the two aborigines to establish the camp behind the look-out ridge, and Emma did not see him, until lunch. They hadn't waited for him, and Karl had just said that the previous evening had been better than the blood-and-gutzers, when he joined them.

"Must have been working this morning," Matt said, heavily humorous.

"Working! I never work! So my Chief insists. Looking forward to the social function, Emma?"

Emma appeared doubtful and said so. Karl said not to worry about the house and farm as he would be working near by.

"It's going to be all right, Emma," Bony told her. "We're all going to be nice and gossipy and give them what they hope to get and take what we hope to take. We should leave about two o'clock, meaning that you will be ready at two-thirty, and we arrive at three."

"We been wonderin' where you found that suitcase," Karl said, hopefully, and Bony burst into laughter.

"Seems pretty cheerful this morning, don't he, Emma?" remarked Matt. "Must be sparking on all six. Says nothing about where he found the case, nothing about how he got it out of the burnt tree, and nothing about how he got it home on Black Tulip."

"Now, now!" Bony reproved, mockingly. "When I present our friend all nicely manacled for Sasoon, if I told you every little unimportant detail you would not then say: 'How did you do it, Nat? How clever you must be, Nat. Oh, Nat, you are just wonderful.' "

"I told you he was sparking on all six," grumbled Matt.

Bony was a little more communicative when driving Emma and her husband down to the Inlet.

"Where I found the case doesn't matter. I raised it with a length of fencing wire. I carried it by the handle on Black Tulip. No horse ever hated a suitcase more. What a name to give a steed with wings to him. Breckoff says he prefers horses to office work, so he'll now have the chance to show off. Thanks, Matt, for providing them with horses."

"Anything you want, Nat. What are they riding after?"

"To seek Marvin's tracks by riding the boundaries of the joint properties. We don't know yet if Marvin is here or has left. We can proceed only on the hope that he is. Now, here we are, and there is old Jeff Rhudder and his wife waiting at the gate to receive us."

Emma did not remember ever having the door of a car or truck opened for her until this day. Now for the second time it was held open for her, and on this occasion the strong brown hand clasped lightly about her arm conveyed a message reminding her to be cautious. Then she was advancing to the couple inside the gateway, and Bony closed the door and followed after her and Matt. She was dressed in a cool green frock. Her face was slightly flushed and her dark eyes were bright.

"Well, here you are, and a pleasant day, too," the stout, flamboyantly-dressed Mrs Sarah Rhudder said in greeting. "A long time ago since you were down here last time, Emma. How are you?"

Waiting for the preliminary greetings to be exchanged, Bony paused to close the gate and note swiftly the garden massed with flowers without the orderliness of plan. Then he was looking into weak brown eyes set widely apart in a heavy pale face, and registering the square determined chin. Sarah offered neither hand, and he bowed slightly, saying how nice it was of her to ask him down. First impression: cold water at the bottom of a well.

Then he was stepping forward to meet old Jeff. The man was six feet tall. He was gaunt rather than thin. His hair, white and wavy, rose above the high and narrow forehead like that of an aboriginal medicine man who wears a snake-skin to keep it so. The features were spare still, weathered like long-exposed jamwood. He was wearing an old-fashioned dress-shirt with stiff cuffs and a wing collar under the waistcoat which matched his trousers. The tie was black. First impression: a storm-defiant karri tree.

Jeff Rhudder held forward his left hand, the right about the bone handle of a stick. His grip was firm. He managed a smile, and the smile lit his grey eyes in their frames of pain, and widened his mouth as though smiling had never been spontaneous. Old! At sixty-seven he was as old as Australia's Front Door.

"Excuse the left, Nat. Touch of sciatica. Don't mind us calling you Nat. These parts are out of the Mister Country. Like up your way, I suppose."

"Well, if it isn't Nat it's the flaming boss, or the chief galah," Bony responded laughingly. The two women had gone on to the wide veranda steps, and Jeff turned to Matt Jukes, saying:

"How-ya, Matt?" with a faint trace of diffidence.

"Not too bad. How-ya, Jeff."

Their host led the way along the neat path, walking slowly and obviously lame. He and Matt began to talk of cattle prices, and Bony was able to note what he was now seeing. At intervals on either side the path, sections of a whale's vertebrae supported large red pots. At the veranda steps the ribs of a whale formed a high arch, and like the pot-stands they were grey and obviously of great age. When Jeff needed time to negotiate the steps, Bony gazed about at the bright garden and the front of the house which had been modernized, seeing how it faced the Inlet and the west wind. To the left of the steps was a bench of blackwood, and either side the bench, affixed to a support, was the figurehead of a ship. They were two magnets.

"The one on your left came from a vessel named *Hesperus*. She came ashore in 1838. The other one was brought ashore too. A three-master, full-rigged Dutchman, named *Van Doren*. Wrecked here in 1818."

Old Jeff spoke from the veranda railing above, and looking up, Bony said the relics were indeed unique.

"Farther back still the East Indian traders often piled up on this coast," Jeff continued. "Having sailed past the Cape of Good Hope they sailed due east for 2,000 miles before turning north to the Indies and China, but in those days navigation was chancy and they sailed on east to come ashore either side of Australia's Front Door. Come on up, and I'll show you something."

Mounting the steps, Bony heard Emma say: "Oh yes, we do want rain, don't we!" And Sarah Rhudder's reply: "But then it never rains but it dampens lovers and flowers."

Old Jeff was waiting for Bony and directed him to the wall of the house against which stood surprising items. There were such things as copper cooking-pots, a ship's bell, a horn-lantern, a cannon, and of all strange things a bird perch mounted on a thin column based in what could be lead.

"Some of the things picked up by my ancestors," explained old Jeff. "Mostly found in the caves where the survivors must have lived until the blacks got 'em. That bird's perch must have a tale to tell. The cross stick is solid gold, the column is made of copper, and the bottom plate is pure silver. I don't tell that to everyone."

"A bird perch of gold and copper and silver!" echoed Bony. "How extraordinary!"

"My son, Marvin ..." Jeff faltered. "My son invented the story behind the perch. Seems that in the days of Captain Kidd and Morgan, and those gentlemen of the seas, one of 'em had a parrot. The parrot was a knowing bird, and it told the captain tales about the mate planning a mutiny. The captain had the mate hanged from the yard-arm, and rewarded the parrot with a golden perch. That sound likely to you?"

"Quite. In those days precious metals were used, not reburied in vaults."

"There's other treasures inside. You look at them sometime. Excuse me now. I must sit down. You take that chair. Smoke if you want. How's the country up your way?"

It was all very pleasant. The light wind came from the Inlet, and the smell of algae was almost banished by the scents of the garden flowers. The three men talked of cattle and sheep, and no personal question was asked of Bony by Jeff, the perfect host. Emma and Mrs Rhudder talked over a tablecloth the large woman was working on, and in the middle of speaking about a plague of kangaroos having dire effect on ground feed needed by the stock, Bony heard Mrs Rhudder say, carelessly:

"To the ants all grass blades are tall, Emma."

Recalling her variation of an old cliché, Bony thought it odd she should be prone to quotations, as neither voice nor subject matter so far gave the impression that she was educated. That she was talking as though against Emma could be attributed to the pleasure of the visit. In fact, the atmosphere on this charming veranda was certainly not supporting the supposition that their hunted son was hiding in the pantry.

Into these wayward thoughts intruded a slim dark-eyed man of perhaps thirty years. He appeared quietly. He was dressed in gaberdine slacks and open-neck sports shirt, and old Jeff could not deny him. Matt and he rose, and the new-comer was introduced as Mark, "Our youngest son." Mark's handshake was soft. His dark eyes were searching before they became reserved. He greeted Bony coolly, and Matt casually, and Emma with "How-ya, Emma," before sitting on a straight-back chair as though he intended not to stay long.

As they talked, Mark Rhudder appeared to listen intently, but Bony became sure he was not at all interested in what his father and Matt said, and very much so in what he, Bony, had to say. His first question was to Bony.

"Just where is your place, Nat?"

"East of a property called Narndee, which is east of Mount Magnet." Bony added the statistics of his 'property', viz., area, carrying capacity, bores, etc., and was again sure, this time, that Mark was memorizing the figures.

Mark, he felt, further tested him, saying:

"Then you can't be far off the Number One Vermin Fence."

"No, right against it with my south-west paddock."

"Read somewhere about that Fence, Nat. Goes from north to south right across the State, doesn't it?"

"That's right. All of 1,130 miles from the Southern Ocean to the Indian Ocean at the Eighty Mile Beach." Old Jeff wanted to know if the Great Fence served its purpose of keeping kangaroos, emus and other vermin from the western agricultural areas, and the subject continued with them until as silently as Mark appeared there came Sadie Stark to ask Mrs Rhudder:

"Shall we have tea now?"

"Of course, Sadie," agreed Sarah, and stood. "Oh, you have met Mr Bonnar, Nat, haven't you?"

Across the intervening space, Bony bowed slightly and smiled, saying:

"Yes, it was the other evening. How are you, Miss Stark?"

"Oh, not Miss Stark. Sadie. We're still outside the Mister Country, Nat," he was reproved by his hostess. "Come along, everyone. A cup of tea will be nice."

Old Jeff had to take his own time to leave the veranda, and Bony considered himself fortunate because Jeff paused to tell him that the front door of mahogany came from a wreck in his grandfather's day, and that the iron hinges were found in a cave three miles westward of Australia's Front Door. The hall was spacious and they paused to examine the glass-topped specimen cases set against three of the walls. One case held coins: doubloons ducats, guineas and American gold dollars found, so Jeff said, by his ancestors who lived here at the Inlet. The other cases were filled with shells, hundreds of them, from great conch-shells to the minute specimens no larger than Egyptian scarabs, and of all colours.

"They're Sadie's," Jeff whispered as though it were a secret. "She collects shells. Been doing it for years. You get her to explain 'em sometime. Then normally he said: "Yes, all those muskets and cutlasses and dress swords, and harpoons, the bullet moulds and the powder horns, they all were washed ashore, or came ashore with the half-drowned mariners. The coins, though, my father told me they came ashore in the pockets of drowned men, and his grandfather told him that while the gold came the family would prosper. It has, too. But the gold stopped years ago."

"They must have been tough characters in those days, Jeff."

"Not only tough, Nat. In those days there were new worlds to conquer and they had the spirit to conquer them. Not like the men of today. My son Marvin, now. He could of ... We'll leave him, Nat. He's a sword in my vitals. Come again, soon, and we'll talk about those pages of history hanging there on the walls."

Following Jeff to the large dining-room, Bony felt pity for this man condemned to live out his last days in bitterness, and sorrow. If Jeff was harbouring his atrocious son, if he had sent him on his way more greatly in sorrow than in furious anger, who was he with three almost faultless sons to cavil or criticize?

The dining-room picture windows faced to the northwest, taking in the entire Inlet and the rising, green hills beyond. There was a telescope on a brass stand and Bony flashed a glance to the hills and picked out the ridge where, he hoped, one of the aborigines was now on observation duty. Like the hall, this room contained specimen cases and some of the furniture was so antique and so beautifully kept that his love of beauty was quickened.

He sat between Mrs Rhudder and Sadie Stark, and soon had to stand again when presented to Mrs Stark, tall, thin, alert with grey-blue eyes which looked steadily at him, probing, examining.

"I see you are quite a conchologist," he said to Sadie, and she, glancing sideways at him, keeping her face tilted to the table, reciprocated by nodding. He had the impulse to force her chin upward to see into her eyes, and perhaps her mind, and the impulse vanished when she turned to him and did for a moment meet his eyes.

"I've always been interested in pretty things," she told him, her mouth widening in a smile which reminded him strongly of the Madonna, aloof, mysterious, knowing all things ... especially men.

He was drawn into the subject of fishing, and Mark added his warning about fishing alone off the rocks, saying how necessary it was to have a companion to watch for the sneaker.

"My word, yes!" he was backed by his mother. "If you must rock fish, Nat, have someone with you. Call on us, and someone will go with you, and show you the best places, too."

He told them they were very kind, and that he would like to accept their offer one day before having to return home. Old Jeff repeated his invitation to come again, spend the day fishing and the evening yarning over dinner and a drink.

Luke did not make his appearance, and Bony wondered where he might be, as no car had passed the Jukes's homestead for Timbertown, and no car had left this place since they had been there.

Driving home later in the afternoon, Matt said almost explosively:

"That Marvin's not about here any longer. I'll bet on it. They're all too easy in their minds. He's cleared off, and they're glad about it. Even old Jeff was better than usual."

During the next mile Bony continued to be introspective, and then he asked:

"Mrs Rhudder has a queer way of expressing herself.

"When we were leaving and I said I'd like to hook and land a two-hundred pound kingfish she said: 'Remember: "Ambition is the main source of evil." ' On the veranda she said that to the ants all grass blades are tall. She didn't seem to me as being a reader of books."

It was Emma who answered him.

"That's from Marvin. He was always saying things like that." She was silent for a space, and then said: "Used to remind me of a book we had about Oscar Wilde. More than once I thought he was trying to copy him."

Chapter Twelve

The Six Scents

Care had to be taken with binoculars against sunlight. Care had to be taken with a camp fire which might smoke. A third precaution to be rigidly adopted was to avoid headlights when travelling between the Jukes's homestead and the camp at the Ridge. A vehicle moving up a steep grade throws its light beams into the sky.

Bony rode a quiet horse to Ridge Camp shortly after returning from the party at Rhudder's Inlet. Lew was on duty. Outwardly this aborigine looked seventy when at fifty. He was stocky, tough, and deliberate in movements. His face was lined. His teeth being false were brilliant. His hair was white and clipped short, and his moustache was full and draped his chin. He had the glasses trained on Bony long before the latter sighted the camp.

"Constable Breckoff and young Fred not back yet?" asked Bony.

"Not yet," replied Lew, voice accentless. "Might be late. About fourteen miles each way."

"What have you seen?"

"Well, the Constable said I had to remember everything." Lew smiled faintly as though he could not be expected to be a tape-machine, or something of the kind. Glancing at his wrist-watch, he said: "No one left the place all morning. Come half-past one Luke Rhudder went fishing. Must have gone fishing with a hand line 'cos he didn't have a rod. Ten to three a car went down to the house and Matt Jukes and his Missus and you got out. You all had a yabber with Jeff and his missus in the garden. They went on up the veranda and you stayed a bit looking at the figureheads. Then you went on up and sat on the veranda for a bit. Mark came and sat, too. Then someone, I couldn't see because she kept in the shadow, must have said for you all to go inside. You all came out twenty after five and drove up home. You had just hit the scrub when Luke came up from the beach, and went home. Coming back he didn't have his gunny-sack."

First impression: normal for an aborigine of Lew's age and time, and early background in association with one much later in life. Bony was delighted with him.

"So, on returning from the beach he didn't have his gunny-sack?"

"That's right." Lew's black eyes steadily appraised the blue eyes of the man he had been told was a big-feller policeman. His eyes gave nothing of his thoughts, and they received nothing from Bony.

"You can hand-line down there?" asked Bony.

"Yes. But Luke had more than a hand line in the sack. Could be he had grub and a thermos. The sack didn't look empty to me. And why should he leave a thermos and a hand line on the rocks? What about the fish? Must have caught some fish."

"Sound argument, Lew," Bony agreed, and regarded approvingly the low tent-like sun-shield built with scrub branches, to protect the lens of the binoculars. "You know the house down there?"

"Too right! Been inside, too. I saw the old coins and things, and one day Sadie Stark showed me her shells, wanting me to find one like some she had."

"You know all the Rhudders, eh?"

"Yes. Knew old Jeff's father. A hard case he was, for sure. Great axe man. He tanned my hide once for pinching his apples." Lew chuckled deep in his throat. "Then he give me three of the best, and said I was to ask next time. He only had one eye, and us kids used to say he'd took it out to stick on the back of his head."

"You were down there as a small boy, eh?"

"Us blacks used to camp a couple of miles up the river, as the Inlet was then. The blacks was always camped there. When they got a bigger school at Timbertown the Protector wanted our kids to go there, and we all shifted over to a camp put up by the Government."

"Did you go to school there, too?"

"Me! No. That was only twelve years back."

"Then you'd know Marvin Rhudder and Luke and Mark pretty well."

"Too right! Fred sort of grew up with 'em. Fred's my son. He's with Constable Breckoff. I showed them Rhudder boys how to swim and ride. Showed Sadie Stark, too. Sometimes I worked for old Jeff. Sometimes for Matt Jukes." Lew became pensive, saying: "Sooner be camped on the Inlet than where we are. But the women wants the kids educated. Not like in my old man's days. In them days the men was the boss."

"Still, you are better off, I suppose," prompted Bony.

"Yes, I suppose so. We all has jobs most of the time, and you can't beat education, can you?"

"That's true, Lew. You know why you're here?"

"Constable Breckoff told me and Fred. On the quiet, though."

"D'you know why Marvin is wanted?"

"Bashing women like he bashed Rose Jukes?"

"You know about Rose Jukes?" pressed the surprised Bony.

"Yes. I was working for Matt when it happened, and Matt said I wasn't to say anything but forget it. That's what I done. Not my business."

Not his business; the white man's business. This meeting with Lew was the first gift by Dame Fortune in the current case, and restraining a too eager interest, Bony dug more into fertile ground.

"You'd know Marvin's tracks when you see them again, eh?"

"Never forget 'em," replied Lew, adding with emphasis: "Never."

"How so?"

"Am I telling you anything?" Lew asked, and chuckled again.

"I'm hoping so," answered Bony, responding to Lew's lighter mood.

"My old man was extra special. Him and his cobbers used to go and walk about away over beyond the Leeuwin Light. They were away that time old Jeff's father got his eye knocked out splitting a log for shingles. He wouldn't have no doctor, and there wasn't one handy, anyway. Well, when my old man come home, Jeff's father was getting around wearing one of them eye-shields. He's out after cattle when my old man goes to the house asking for tobacco, and he seen Jeff's father's tracks about the place. He says to Jeff's mother, 'you got a stranger white feller walking around,' and she says there's no stranger. He says there is and that this stranger's got only one eye, the right one."

"Not bad, Lew," murmured Bony, admiringly. "Your father must have been good. But what has all this to do with Marvin?"

"Well, like I told you, my old man was pretty good on tracking. I used to think he could tell what a feller was thinking about by looking at his tracks. More'n once he ordered me not to have anything to do with Marvin, kept on telling me Marvin was a Kedic feller. He'd show me Marvin's tracks and how they told him Marvin was a Kedic." Lew shrugged. "Well, he's a Kedic, all right."

"Meaning he's bad medicine all through? I've heard of the Kedics but by other names. What did your father's people do about them? The same as other aborigines, I suppose?"

"Expect so. Anyway, my old man told me that in his time when they found the tracks of a Kedic feller, they watch him and wait for him to be on his own in the scrub, and then kill him and burn him up. Kedic feller no good. Better kill him before he kills someone. Marvin is a Kedic, he always was. My old man said so, and my old man proved true, didn't he?"

"How do you know Marvin killed someone?" Bony asked. "Bash and rape, yes, but how do you know he killed someone?"

There was mirth in Lew's eyes when he said:

"My old man was good." He patted himself on the chest. "I'm good, too. When I went with the Senior to take casts of Marvin's tracks I saw then he'd killed someone. He did, didn't he?"

Bony nodded. He had heard of such feats, and had tended to discount them as they reduced his own powers of track reading. There was no envy of this aborigine: he could use to advantage his own efforts in hunting down a man. Taking the glasses from Lew, he studied the figure leaving by the garden gate, saw it was Sadie. She had changed from her afternoon frock to a blue blouse and slacks. He asked:

"How did your Fred get along with the Rhudder boys?"

"Little feller with 'em he got along good," Lew replied, and Bony waited for an implication to be explained. He saw Sadie walking beside the Inlet on her way to the sandbar and the beach.

"Fred didn't get along so good when they grew up, eh?"

"No. He didn't like being given the hard thing to do in play, and being called a black bastard by Marvin. There was something else, but Fred would never say. After that he gave 'em away."

"Sadie is off to the beach, with neither gunny-sack nor basket. What kind of a bushman was Marvin when he cleared out that time?"

"Like the rest of 'em," answered Lew. "They was all extra, I'd say. Learned a lot off us."

"And how to smooth out their tracks?"

"They learned that, too."

"Think he'd bluff Fred, or you?"

The low chuckle came and Bony passed the binoculars to the aborigine. With the naked eyes he could see Sadie now walking along the top of the great sand-bar, a fly on a long marble slab.

His horse down at the camp snickered, and he repeated his last question.

"He couldn't bluff me or Fred. Not a hope. Might think he could. He got to thinking us blacks was grit in the eye. Sadie Stark's not going to the beach. She's following the tea-tree along the cliff. Must be going for a walk. Here's Fred and the constable."

"I'll go down. You stay up here and keep the glasses on Sadie."

Constable Breckoff and his tracker were both of the same age, and akin also in physique, tall, tough, and young. The policeman grinned his greeting, for he was tired by the long day's ride spoiled by too much motor-ease, and office-chair. Fred was unsaddling and Bony asked him to take his horse and theirs to water as he would be staying the night. Breckoff took the billy-can to the camp water-tank, and Bony stirred the fire embers and added dry wood.

Rolling a cigarette while waiting for the water to boil, Bony asked how the day had gone with him.

"Nothing in it. We crossed young Rhudder's tracks coming in, and we back-tracked him to the old mill site. We rode wide and right to the coast about six miles east of the homestead. We didn't cut his tracks going out, or the tracks of a horse he could have ridden. Pretty certain he hasn't gone back to Albany, anyway."

"Lew claims that Fred is a good tracker."

"The best."

"Did you tell him or his father that Marvin is wanted for murder?"

"No. The Senior said not to. Only wanted for bashing and rape. Lew know?" Bony told of what Lew had read in the tracks at the creek, and Breckoff whistled admiringly. "They're beauts, eh?"

"They're tops," conceded Bony. "I can't think how Lew would know otherwise. You could spare him for a day?"

"Whatever you say," agreed Breckoff, tossing a half-handful of tea into the boiling water.

"I want him to ride with me along the west boundary to see if Rhudder went by that way to the Leeuwin Light. We'll leave before daylight. I'll tell Lew."

When darkness ended Lew's term of duty on the ridge, he came down to eat with them in the firelight, and to report that Sadie had disappeared into the tea-tree short of Australia's Front Door. When she reappeared half an hour later she was carrying a gunny-sack slung by the strap from a shoulder, and the sack looked quite empty. They discussed the oddity that Luke had gone fishing with a gunny-sack and had returned without it. And the further oddity that Sadie had taken a walk along the cliff without a gunny-sack and had returned with one, empty.

Bony offered no comment, and Breckoff waited on him. It was Fred who, following a period when he teased the firesticks closer together, voiced a solution.

"That bloody Marvin's down there all right, an' all. Luke, he takes tucker to him and leaves the bag, knowing his folk's expecting visitors and won't see him go. And then Sadie she goes along to pick up the empty gunny-sack. The visitors ain't supposed to know nothing."

"How did you know about the visitors to the Inlet today?" queried Bony, and Fred's simple solution of this mystery raised laughter.

"Heard you tell Matt's missus to wear her best clothes for the afternoon party at Rhudders. We was having a cuppa and supper before the Senior left."

"Quick, eh!" Bony said, and Fred smiled with pleasure.

Three o'clock in the morning, Bony roused Lew. They ate breakfast and rode away without disturbing the others, and the new day was lifting high the clear sky when they reached the hut and the yards.

"I want you to go in there, Lew, and sit quiet and use your nose," Bony told his tracker. "Someone's been staying there. Maybe a week or more back. There's a case to sit on."

"There's a well at the back," Lew said, and went to the windlass where Bony heard the cranking and then the aborigine drawing water up his nostrils from his cupped hands, and spitting it out.

"I'm not much good," he told Bony on coming round to the door. "Not like my old father after he'd been on walkabout for a month or more and never a smoke to keep his nose asleep."

He was inside the hut with the door shut for fifteen minutes and on emerging to join Bony, who was standing with the horses, he made his report.

"White man been stopping in there. He had grilled meat to eat off the fire. Perhaps didn't stay long. He had shaving-soap instead of ordinary wash-soap. He was frightened, dead frightened. I could smell him frightened. There was a woman, too. I could smell her. One of 'em had scent, you know the scent they buy at a store. Boronia it's called. More'n likely the woman had the boronia scent. Store scent 'cos the boronia flowering was over months ago."

"I hand it to you, Lew," Bony told him. "I smelled man. I smelled grilled meat. I smelled the shaving soap. The other scent I couldn't name. You beat me there, and you beat me on the smell of fear which I didn't get. Now let's ride and use our eyes."

They rode westward to the boundary and, keeping to outside the fence, they walked their horses, often zigzagging, examining every dry gutter and the edges of every small stream. They looked at every tree they passed by, every bush, and at every stone which could be turned. And when back at camp, Bony knew that Marvin had not left Rhudder's Inlet.

Chapter Thirteen

Bonaparte Is Stern

Bony spent the rest of the day at the police camp, meditating as his maternal ancestors had done, when squatting over a tiny fire and absently pushing the little sticks together. Occasionally he climbed to the ridge to ask if movement had been noted at the Inlet. And when he left on his horse for Matt's homestead he was sure of one thing only, viz., that Marvin Rhudder was still at or in the vicinity of the Inlet. Nothing can induce an aborigine to reach top tracking-form more than dislike of the man to be tracked, and therefore Fred could be completely relied on to be as efficient as his father. Of Lew's efficiency, Bony's long ride that morning had given convincing evidence.

Riding homeward in the growing dusk, again he pondered on the bones he had collected in the short period of his investigation, but the bones he did have he could not build into the skeleton frame of a hypothesis to advance the investigation.

The work done by Lew and Fred, the work additionally done by Breckoff and himself, was good enough on which to found conviction that Marvin was still inside the boundaries of these two Inlet properties. It could be supported by Luke's testing of his assumed background; but it could be opposed by the money and articles in the suitcase found in the tree, by the cheery atmosphere at the Rhudder home, by Luke's decision to return to Perth.

Expert examination of the suitcase and contents might well provide very important leads. On the case itself there could be finger-prints in addition of those of Marvin, and were this so then the finger-prints of everyone at the Inlet would have to be obtained surreptitiously to establish the owner.

Meanwhile, he, Bony, would have to seek for other bones to add to his collection, and other bones might be dug up from the soil of the Rhudder homestead and its people. He would have to cultivate them, and leave to the watchers the larger scene.

He apologized to Emma for being so late, and they forbore to question him on his long absence. He insisted that he wanted only a cup of tea and a buttered scone, knowing he had interrupted the reading which had become the highlight of Karl Mueller's day. After the light supper, and Karl had gone off to bed, he continued to sit with Matt and Emma under the lamp above the table. And it would seem that this was the moment chosen by Sasoon to telephone.

"The old suitcase gives nothing, Nat. The lab reports that inside and outside has been wiped clean. The lab says, too, that only the bloke's prints were found on some of the contents. The money is being further tested, but isn't expected to give much."

"I didn't expect to receive much," Bony replied. "It is important though to know if the money is traced to the bookmaker. I want to keep the gang down here. All right with you?"

"As long as you want 'em. They done any work yet?"

"Just been looking at the scenery, Sam. Very pretty down here, you know."

"It would be. Prettier than here in my ruddy office. How's the folk?"

"As the State will be paying for your call, I'll put Emma on."

There was a pad and pencil which Emma had been using to note down groceries she would be wanting, and Bony tore off a spare page and drew the position of the lightning-blasted tree relative to the hut. The plan he placed before Matt, saying:

"The cross represents a tree which some years ago was struck by lightning. Since the strike a branch which escaped destruction is now a sturdy limb. The top of the tree was burned out to a cinder, and at the bottom of the cylinder was that suitcase. D'you happen to know when the tree was blasted?"

"I know it was before I took over that land," replied Matt. "There's something else I ought to know, too. Wait a minute. It'll come."

Matt was trying hard to quicken memory when Emma hung up and returned to her chair and the memo pad.

"Emma, wasn't there something about a lightning-struck tree long ago? An argument or a row about it over the kids?"

"Yes, that's right. Ted was Starlight, and the others were police troopers. They were gaining on him, so he got up the tree without getting off his horse, kicked his horse on to let the others think he was still riding it. I remember him telling me about it after he got home with his new shirt as black as a kettle and his trousers torn. It seems he went up to the top of the tree, found a hole in it, thought to get inside, and then slipped."

"I remember now," Matt took over. "He didn't think the hole was so deep, and he couldn't get out. Would of stayed there a mighty long time if Marvin hadn't ridden close and heard him yelling. Cripes! That was years ago."

"Then," said Bony, "Marvin would know about that hollow tree?"

"Yes, why?"

"Another little bone, Matt. Tell me this. When you decide to send some cattle to market, do you inform Jeff?"

"Always tell him. He always tells me. It's like this. I muster for to get what fats I want, or can find among the mob. If there's a good number they have to be driven overland. Same goes for Jeff. If we both send cattle, it doesn't want any more men. Sometimes I supply the men, sometimes he does. Saves labour. There might be only half dozen beasts between us to hit a good market, so we pool 'em and send 'em by truck. Saves expenses."

"Excellent!" Bony exclaimed. "And before either mustered you would tell the other about it?"

"We've always done that, Nat. Me and Jeff has always got on smoothly like our fathers did before us. I think I told you so."

"You did. Now if Marvin lived at that hut after returning home, he could receive ample warning through, say, Luke or Mark, even Sadie, that you were going to muster?"

"Easy. Did Marvin live there?"

Bony nodded, and the Jukes waited and watched him roll a cigarette slowly and without once looking at his fingers, and then light it with a match with the same disregard of these physical actions.

"Marvin stayed at that hut for some time," Bony said. "Why he left it for another hiding-place I don't know precisely. It wasn't because of being warned you were going to muster. Probably it was just before he left that he decided to cache his suitcase in that hollow tree. He cleaned the case inside and out to remove his prints, and he did what he could with the things inside. Why? Why do that? Why didn't he take the case to wherever he thought he would be safer? I know, and everyone tells me, there are a thousand safer places for him than that hut."

"Didn't want to be arrested with the case in his possession, might be," Matt suggested, and was countered with:

"Marvin could not be incriminated more than he is by the case and its contents which include the money he murdered for. He wouldn't plant the case there intending to return for the money at some distant date. He'd want the money with him, and he would know that his case would soon rot and the money be quickly pulped when the next heavy rain covered it with water. When he was in that hut he was badly frightened, and I think it was the cause of that fear which drove him out to live in a cliff cave. Now what would frighten him?"

"Nothing," replied Emma quietly. "Marvin wouldn't be frightened of anything."

Bony regarded this small, compact, tidy woman who compared so favourably when set beside Mrs Jeff Rhudder, and even Mrs Sam Sasoon. He had met women like her, and in number they are very few. Emma was wise, and the quality of her wisdom was a gift, not that acquired by experience. She led her husband, ruled him, and doubtless her two children, and not one of them would ever so much as think she led and ruled. She looked at her husband. He was still physically powerful, he was prone to surrender to emotion, and, without realizing it, found comfort in being ruled. Bony smiled, a gentle rueful smile, and said:

"You still have Marvin on his pedestal, eh? You can see him only as he was. Marvin the braggart, the fearless, the natural leader, and oh, so clever, so wonderful a speaker and so marvellous in his ambitions. What you did not see then, and don't now, is that all you did see in him was the façade he built to hide behind. He couldn't hide behind anything from Lew's father, from Lew, and from Fred.

"No one knows about the façade, or shield, he built to protect his inner, his real self, more intimately and closely than Marvin. It has been a wonderful cloak for him to wear, and looking back over his early youth, and early manhood, and later, his dreadful career, he has felt himself completely safe from exposure to his own people, to you, and to the prison authorities and scientific people whom he bamboozled.

"A moment more, Matt. It was likely that on coming home he did not mention his crime of murder. It was even probable that his brother Mark and his mother did not inform his father of his home-coming. But, when Sasoon went there all then knew he was wanted for murder, and eventually one or other of them told him the police were seeking his tracks.

"What then? Marvin would know, of course, that his crime of murder in South Australia meant death by hanging. He knew, equally well, that if and when the police suspected he was here that they would put the aborigines to look for his tracks. He would know that the aborigines set to work after him would include Lew and Fred, who had always been able to see the shrinking fearful thing behind its façade, behind that glorious filthy cloak he wore. It was when in that hut he was told the police were after him that fear of the hangman became naked, so naked, so strong, that the aborigines can smell his fear in that hut to this very day."

Matt and Emma saw him stub out the cigarette-end as though impatient, when actually the normal little chore was absurdly trivial in the balance, compared with the subject occupying his mind.

"One more word," he asked of them. "In his extremity Marvin Rhudder would now be capable of walking into his old home and slaughtering his own parents. He is capable of walking into this house and killing anyone found here whom he thinks might oppose him or his desires. I believe he will not visit his home or come here, and I believe it because he is now too frightened to leave the dark hole in which he hides. I have pulled him from his pedestal so that you may take reasonable steps to safeguard yourselves."

Matt abruptly stood, and anger flared from his blazing eyes. "If he came here I'd shoot him on sight," he cried. "I never put him on a pedestal. I don't forget what he did to our Rose."

"You don't even now understand what I have been trying to do, to tell you, Matt," Bony went on calmly. "You still see Marvin sauntering to this house and asking for food, or something. You cannot see him as I do. You say you'd shoot him on sight, and I say he wouldn't give you the opportunity to see him over your gunsight.

"I can do nothing for the people at the Inlet. I can, and do, ask you to adopt reasonable precautions like locking the doors, and having a little dog to sleep here in the living-room. And, Matt, keep close to Emma always. I cannot be here with you. Now I know for certain that Marvin hasn't left, that he is still at the coast, I have to go after him."

Matt sat down as though weary, and Emma said:

"Thank you, Nat. We were a tiny bit blind, weren't we? Don't worry about us any more. And now it's so late would you like a cup of tea before going to bed?"

The look of severity on his face and in his eyes gave place to a beaming smile.

"Thou knowest a man's weaknesses, O Emma."

Chapter Fourteen

The Stalking Sneaker

The night was cool and quiet, and the scents of Emma's flowers and those of the forest behind the homestead were sentient beings vying to enter Bony's room. A dog growled, and Bony was instantly awake. Another dog barked and the other supported its alarm. They announced the coming of a car from the Inlet.

In green striped pyjamas, Bony slipped from the house and ran the short distance to the track to Timbertown. It was only then that he heard the sound of the vehicle, and was aware it would be travelling at twenty five miles an hour over this unmade road. It was fast enough to cause his haste.

Its headlights shot beams into the faint mist above the trees, then it gilded the top of the karri tree, finally to glare on the trackside tree behind which he had taken cover. The car came on with its engine purring, did not take the turn off to the homestead, passed Bony with the instrument lights switched off. He could not identify the driver, but the silhouette of the car in addition to the rear number-plate proved it to be that owned by Luke Rhudder.

In the living-room he found Matt also in pyjamas.

"Was that Luke? Said he was going home today, didn't he?"

"It was his car, Matt. Mind me telephoning? Sorry to disturb you. Three o'clock! Must be hoping to get up to Perth before the real heat of the day there."

"Poor old Sam," Matt said, and grinned.

"Now what!" said poor old Sam. "That you, Nat?"

"Luke's car has just passed. Couldn't see who was driving, or if he had any passengers. Remember he told his wife he'd be coming home today."

"Yes. Think he's worth checking?"

"I was going to suggest it," Bony said mockingly, and Sasoon chuckled and came fully awake. "Don't report until six. I'm going back to bed."

"And they say a policeman's life is all beer and bash."

Bony went back to bed, and immediately slept. The dogs settled and the many perfumes took over the night. Until half past three when the dawn touched the sky, and a little wind came from the sea. It was then that the birds decided on revenge for being rudely disturbed.

In a cedar-tree just beyond Emma's detached laundry a cock butcher-bird practised one note several times, before rendering the first of four distinct melodies. It was as though this small imp of a bird knew that Bony had earned a night's sleep, because he kept at his repertoire until another of his kind entered into competition.

The several magpies in the karri tree began to contribute their warbling to the orchestra, producing the sweetest notes in Nature, each musician playing with all stops out and doing his damnedest. The performance was unique, unforgettable, lovely enough to stir the heart of a goanna. But why, oh why, at half past three in the morning?

Bony clawed the sleep from his eyes and went to the living-room where he filled a kettle and put it on the primus for quick boiling. He opened the door and stood there. The light was filling the sky with pearls and opals. The birds' music stopped. There was complete silence for half a minute. Then several kookaburras cackled and screamed their laughter at him, and he had either to shake his fist or laugh back at them, and did neither as his mind was occupied by the worm in the apple of this Garden of Eden. A rooster crowed, and that did interrupt his thinking with the extraneous thought that the rooster had crowed many times this morning without being noted.

"Talk about Alfred and the cakes!" exclaimed Emma. "You've let the kettle boil dry."

Turning into the house he saw Emma in a bright kimono, and holding the ruined tin kettle by a fork under the handle.

"I am sorry," he told her. "I was thinking, really."

"That's what King Alfred did, but I won't scold you, Nat. We've another kettle."

Matt appeared, yawning. He kicked off his slippers and pulled on elastic-side boots, and muttered something about the damned birds, and that he'd shoot 'em for sure. Emma said he'd made that threat every summer for many years, and he went outside for kindling to fire the range.

There were two telephone calls that morning. The first was from Sasoon who said he had stopped Luke at the railway crossing and that Luke had no passenger with him in the car, in the boot, or on the roof. Luke had demanded an explanation and was told he was unlucky by travelling so early as all cars were being searched for possum skins. Then shortly after seven the second call was answered by Emma. It was Mrs Rhudder saying that Jeff was out of sorts and being difficult, and would Nat Bonnar care to go rock-fishing with Sadie? Low tide would be a little after ten, and Nat would be welcome to lunch and would be so kind if he would talk Jeff out of his moods and pains and aches. Bony nodded his consent, and Emma said he would be down there in time to fish the tide.

The dawn wind had been frighted away by the bird orchestra, and when Bony stopped his car outside the Rhudder garden-gate, the surface of the Inlet was sheet metal and all the water birds merely toy ornaments. From the ocean came the low thuds and sharper slaps by the surf to rock faces.

Sadie Stark appeared with a heavy gunny-sack slung from a shoulder and carrying two stout rods. She seemed surprised when Bony hurried forward to relieve her of the gear.

"This is being very nice of you," he said. "How is Jeff?"

"Awake most of the night, and grumpy this morning."

The gear he pushed into the boot, the lid weight keeping the rods from sliding out, and at the wheel he expressed the hope that they would catch a record fish, asking what species of fish they might land.

"Kingfish," she replied. "We must be there at dead low, for kingfish come by soon after the tide turns."

She was wearing an old and patched pair of dungaree slacks, a blue guernsey and rubber sand-shoes. Bony wore clothes not much better but equally serviceable.

Neither bothered with a hat. They left the car at the pinch between the Inlet and the coast dunes, and having gathered the rods and the gunny-sack, Bony followed after Sadie.

Of about his height, now verging on thirty, her body had the resilience and hardness of contours of a woman much younger. Even in sand-shoes she walked with the elegant freedom of a mountain lass, her back straight and shoulders strong, and her legs springy and confident. She halted at the seaward edge of the bar for him to overtake and stand beside her. Here she scanned the coast to the rock-bound west and the mighty line of dunes stretching in an arc to the east. Without looking at him, she said:

"Jeff has the idea that millions of years ago those dunes weren't there, and that the sea rolled inland to form a great bay. Now only the river and what's called the Inlet is left of what was a bay. Have you angled for kingfish?"

"Oh yes!" replied Bony, regarding the waves breaking in long and seemingly solid rolls of water on the stones far below the bar.

"It's a good morning for them. We might get a whopper. I think we'll try from Ted's Rock."

"Ted's Rock! Which one is that?"

"The one standing out to sea beyond that mountain of seaweed. We can get to it along the rock-bars, but must be off it before the tide is half in. Or stay there for hours waiting for the tide to go down."

"You're the boss, Sadie. A good size kingfish would be worth going for."

She went down by the harder slope of the bush-covered dune, and at the narrow strip of coarser sand again waited for him. Skirting the dunes for several hundred yards brought them to a wide area of sand from which the tide had receded, and thus they found walking easier and were able to proceed together.

"You named that rock Ted's Rock," he said. "Is that the rock where Ted Jukes was washed off?"

"It was more than an ordinary sneaker. Underwater volcanic action must have raised the wave. We could see that by the damage it did to the coast. It was a day like today, and Ted didn't have anyone watching for him."

"It must have been a blow for Matt and Emma."

"A blow to all of us," he was corrected. "See this hill of weed? Fascinates me. The sea gathers it and builds it, and leaves it alone for weeks, perhaps months, and then the waves will smash into it and carry it all away. Only to bring it all back and build again some other place."

Passing by the seaward face of the mass rising in places to fifty feet or more and covering several acres (it was the home of thousands of small crabs, orange in colour), Bony said:

"I've seen a seaweed mountain, although not as big as that one, south of Geraldton. The same kind of crabs, too. Have you ever been up to Geraldton?"

"No, never farther north than Perth." The girl walked in silence for a few minutes. Then: "I've always wanted to visit the Barrier Reef, and places like that. But I never shall."

"Wrong way of looking at the future," Bony said, smilingly.

"I know what I know, Nat. Had my hand read once at a fair in Timbertown. Woman told me I'd never travel, would always stay at home and die an old maid. D'you believe in palmistry?"

"No," replied Bony, and forbore to mention that he believed wholeheartedly in pedestry in telling of the past.

They came to a rising shelf of rock and began to climb Ted's Rock at the shore side, Sadie leading the way to the summit which was fairly flat and weathered. At this elevation of something like two hundred feet, the sea looked as flat as the water of the Inlet. It was unbroken save where the waves met the coast rocks and rose high to crash on the narrow beaches.

They thundered dully against the base of Ted's Rock, seemingly barely rising until one looked attentively at them.

"Must be deep caverns down below," Bony surmised. "The backwash is late. Matt said there's generally a sneaker at the change of low tide. What causes them, d'you know?"

"Well, Jeff says that the rock-bars under the sea are like arms and when the tide or a particular series of waves surge landward the narrowing arms hump them into one big one. I've read of other theories, but Jeff's is better than any of those. Now you'd better prepare your gear."

Bony fitted a heavy line-loaded reel to one of the rods and taking the line up through the guides knotted it to the thin wire trace and to that expertly knotted the hook. He was aware that his companion was watching, and knew she couldn't fault him. When taking the second reel from the sack, she said:

"You fish: I'll watch today. You go down to that ledge and cast." She indicated a narrow ledge midway to the water, where the water appeared to be far below the ledge. "When you've tired a fish you'll have to take him to the end of the ledge, where it's sheer, and then reel him up. Get that?"

"Yes. That's clear."

"And if you hear me shout you must come up at once."

"Very well." Glancing at her he found himself able to look directly into her grey eyes flecked with brown, and now they seemed to take the colour of the sea and appear almost purple. In them was that calm and still expression so often associated with eyes habitually gazing at the sea or across the desert, and they did not change when he smiled before picking up the bait-tin and beginning the descent to the ledge. When next he saw her she was sitting and looking out to sea, her hands on her lap, her body as motionless as the hands. He failed to recall having ever met a woman like Sadie Stark.

The ledge was wider than it appeared from the top, and he found plenty of room to stand comfortably and make his cast. Fifty feet below him the water was unbroken, coming in powerfully to mount over the next incoming wave. The nylon line went deep before fading out.

The kingfish is rightly named. In speed and power in ratio to weight it reduces the trout to a mere tiddler. There is no pause in its dash to take the bait, some say at sixty miles an hour. Bony set himself in readiness to apply the reel-brake gradually, to play the fish and tire it being the first demand on skill.

Yes, Sadie Stark was a new experience, and now at this third meeting he received the impression that she had read every book in the world, that she had lived for a thousand years, that she had dissected the mind of ten thousand men and knew with unshakeable conviction that all of them were children.

The tide was now at low water, and there would be a pause of a few seconds. He remembered that Matt had said the sneaker invariably came in behind the Door, following this tidal pause. He gazed out to sea. The surface out from the rock was flat and unbroken. The sea was blue and placid. There, seemingly miles distant was a thin streak which he put down as an oil slick from a passing ship.

The lead sinker was being moved by the currents over the sand-ribs deep in the sea, and when there came up the line a slow but determined tug, he lifted the bait, and the weight told of a crayfish attack. He reeled in line to defeat the crayfish, let it flow back again, and he was satisfied that he had thwarted the crustacean when he noted again the oil slick. It was less than two hundred yards distant.

The sun was glinting on the shoreward slope of a racing wave, and it was now glittering on the facets of the disturbed summit of the whale-back. Bony glanced up at Sadie, and she was sitting as he had last seen her. Then the wave was barely a hundred yards away, and then the water directly below began magically to rise.

Spinning about he began a mad scrabble up the steep rock slope, holding the rod by one hand and having to use the other to assist him. The reel started to scream as line was torn from it. The girl began to shout. It seemed that he made no headway, that as he climbed the rock was turning over and down to the sea. Under an arm, between his feet, he saw the ledge sink into white foam. The hubbub of the girl's shouting and the screaming reel became tiny and silly as background to that rock-engulfing wave.

Chapter Fifteen

The Local Mona Lisa

Chaos and cacophony churned about Bony; the hissing of water cascading down the faces of Ted's Rock; the dwindling scream of the reel; the shouting of the girl; and far away, the thundering of the sneaker raging ashore.

He found a place to stand upright and turn again to the sea. From a yard below his feet the rock was pure white and jet black, down and down to the smother of foam. The reel stopped. The line stretching far away to meet the water slacked abruptly, telling that the fish had slipped the hook or was engaged with second thoughts.

"Come on up, Nat! Come up at once!" Sadie urged, and he began to reel in the line.

He wasn't going to permit that fool of a woman to hear his rasping breathing, to see in his eyes the waning light of fear, to note with scorn the trembling of his lips and hands. Mooning there like a love-sick teenager, and she an experienced watcher for the sneaker. He'd take his time winding in the line, and watch for himself. Then came the sudden weight and sudden renewal of the reel scream, and now, by heck, he'd stay and fight the fish.

The heat left his body, and the anger turned to a pebble in the sea of his mind, now given to calculation. The fish was straight out from the rock, and the angle of the line raised it from being cut against the rock ledge. It was a trier, and as yet untired. It hauled with irresistible power against the reel-brake, but now, bereft of speed, it could gain only a yard a minute.

The fish tried another tactic. It sliced to and fro, to and fro, and Bony stopped it at the end of each run, at the same time bringing it closer and closer. When the line came near the cutting rock-edge, he began to descend to the ledge, and Sadie cried to him not to go down the wet surface.

Still holding, not giving the fish an inch, he reached the ledge and continued the fight, and, in view of the final manoeuvre, played it to complete exhaustion. It was comparatively easy to draw it to the sheer drop at the end of the ledge, and this was where the real work began.

Immediately the fish was brought to the surface, the rod bucked and bowed, and the testing of the rod and line became fearsome when the fish was lifted clear. Bony waited for the fish to expire, bracing himself against its weight. Above, the girl was silent. A gull cried, and other than that cry there was only the sound of the rollers thudding in under the rock.

Raising the long thick-bodied slate-grey fish occupied him a full ten minutes, and when it appeared over the rock lip, Bony could have shouted, for it weighed at least forty pounds. He was on the verge of gasping for air when he got it to the top, and laid the rod on it and sat down to roll a cigarette.

"Nice fish, eh!" he said, not looking at Sadie. "What d'you think? Forty-odd pounds?"

She offered no comment, and having lit the cigarette he saw her sitting again, her hands in her lap, her face tilted down and hidden from him.

"What's the matter?" he asked her.

"I thought the sea was going to get you. I should have warned you sooner. I was watching a seal, not the sea."

"I was watching the sea. I saw the wave coming in. I would have been mad if this fish had got away. Isn't he a beauty!"

"Yes. But it was my fault. The sneaker could easily have grabbed you. I was sure it would. You don't seem to know how near it was behind you."

"Don't I?" laughed Bony. "You're not telling me a thing. Anyway, it didn't, so cheer up. When I took the reels from the gunny-sack did I feel a thermos flask?"

She was looking at him, and her eyes were the colour of the kingfish. Her mouth widened, the lips trembled slightly, and she said:

"You are very generous not to scold me. Marvin would have knocked me down. Yes, there's a thermos of tea and sandwiches. Let me."

Sadie produced the flask and an enamel jug, and she was groping into the bag when she said vexatiously:

"Damn! There should have been another cup. I'll drink from the flask cup. You unwrap the sandwiches."

She insisted that he take the mug, and when they were eating, he said:

"Everyone says this coast is dangerous, and now I believe it. You mentioned Marvin. Fine-looking fellow from the picture of him I was looking at the other evening. So was Ted Jukes. A great pity about Ted. Yes, I can realize clearly now how dangerous this coast is."

She was looking at the flask near her foot when she spoke.

"That wasn't an ordinary sneaker today. I've never seen it come just like that, real sneaky. Still, I was supposed to watch. Would you ... would you say nothing about it at the house?"

"As you wish. These sandwiches are delicious."

"And if Jeff wants to talk about Marvin, would you be careful? You see, Marvin has blighted their lives, all our lives. Rose didn't mention him, I suppose?"

Bony shook his head and gazed out to sea where a white painted liner was passing on its way to Freemantle. She was still looking downward when he flashed a glance at her.

"No, Rose said nothing about any of the Rhudders, excepting that they had a boat and lived here for generations. Emma did say he's the prodigal son and has been away for years. Prodigal sons do give parents worry and grief, don't they?"

"Marvin has done so." For a moment she looked directly at him before pretending interest in the ship. "Perhaps you should know a little about him to be on your guard if Jeff brings him up. He was the most wonderful boy who ever lived. Big and fine and handsome. There was nothing he couldn't do, and nothing he wouldn't dare. School and college work came as easy to him as asking for another cup of tea. Yes, there's plenty more in the flask. He was going to become a minister. Then he fell sick and he's always been sick."

"Mentally sick?"

"Yes, mentally sick," Sadie went on. "Been in gaol half a dozen times. Assault and robbery and all that. The police are looking for him because he broke his bond, and they thought he might have come home. He did too."

"Oh!" mildly exclaimed Bony. "Was the fatted calf killed?"

He could detect the faint note of urgency when she said:

"Have you any sons? I seem to remember you said you did. If one of them, say, the one you loved most, the clever one, threw love to the winds and broke into vicious crime after crime, would you make a fuss of him when he came home?"

"You pose a difficult problem. My eldest son is a medical missionary working in the Islands. He's brilliant. He won scholarship after scholarship. I'm tremendously proud of him. If he fell sick as Marvin Rhudder seems to have done, I hardly know what I'd do. H'm! I wouldn't make a fuss of him, but probably I'd help him ... if help were possible."

"You had a good education, didn't you?" she pressed, her eyes meeting his.

"That's so. Haven't made much use of it, though. Having gained my interest in the Rhudder prodigal you must tell me more. What happened when he returned home?"

"You won't tell anyone, even Matt and Emma Jukes?"

"Very well. Actually it doesn't concern me. Why do you want to tell me? Don't if you'd rather not."

"Well, I think you should know because you'll be meeting Jeff again this afternoon. He might ask some leading questions, knowing you're with the Jukes, and suspecting sometimes that Marvin came home. You see, we kept it from him. Marvin was in the tool room at the machinery shed one morning when I was collecting the eggs. He wanted to know how Jeff would accept him, and I said I'd have to find out what his mother thought about it, as Jeff had threatened a hundred times to shoot him. Not that he would, but you know how ill he is. We, that is his mother and I, said he was not to see his father and he wasn't to stay. He said he'd broken his bond in Sydney. He said he was tired of being like a hunted animal. He said he wanted to go straight, but even his mother knew he'd never do that.

"Anyway, he refused to go away, and we sent up for Luke, Luke being stronger than Mark. Well, Luke came down and ordered Marvin off the property, for a start. He had Marvin go and live for the time being at the old hut on the other side of the Inlet, and we took blankets and food to him, and bought different clothes for him. In the end Luke gave him some money and he went away, after telling Luke and me he'd slip through the forest and thumb a ride to Perth and get to Freemantle, and take a ship abroad.

"That's the way it began and ended, and Jeff doesn't know anything. We don't want him to know, ever. He's been hurt badly enough, and besides, he's always been kind and generous to my mother and me. So you'll remember, and keep off Marvin should he ask questions?"

"All right," consented Bony. "You say he suspects that Marvin came home. What raised his suspicions?"

"Luke coming home, we think. You see, Luke and his wife and children were down over the Christmas and New Year, and then he came this last time alone. To make it worse, the other day the police came asking if we'd seen anything of Marvin. After that, Luke insisted on Marvin going away and keeping away."

"A tragedy, indeed," murmured Bony. "Must be a terrible burden on his mother. Yes, I'll be most careful if Jeff asks lead-questions."

"Thank you, Nat."

Sadie stood and gathered the mug and flask into the sack, and Bony dismantled the rod, line and reel. He cut a length of cord-line to loop through the gills of the great fish to carry it, and they were ready to leave when the girl said:

"What would make Jeff think he could pump you is that Emma's very friendly with Elsie, the policeman's wife. Emma might have told you something or other what Sam had told her. That could be the way Jeff's thinking. And now Marvin's gone away again, we all want the whole affair forgotten."

"Yes, of course, I can see that," Bony said gravely. "It does happen that Matt and Emma are genuinely concerned about Jeff's health. Matt told me how close in friendship they've always been. I can understand how they wouldn't want to discuss the Rhudder affairs with me, being a complete stranger. So don't worry. I'll be careful."

She nodded her thanks, and her eyes were bright as, without evasion, they sought his and apparently emphasized the head nod. Glancing at her watch, she said:

"We must get on home. Nearly lunch-time, and I've to take mother up to Timbertown this afternoon to do some shopping. I'll carry the gear. You'll have enough to do with the fish. He's a beauty, isn't he?"

In the car, Bony insisted that the fish be halved, and on arriving at the garden gate he was instructed to drive into the rear yard and to the meat-house. There with a sharp knife he filleted the fish despite Sadie Stark's protests that she could do it quite well. For the second time, she asked him to be silent about the adventure with the sneaker.

"I'd never hear the end of it, if they knew."

Old Jeff was on the veranda waiting to receive the visitor, and at once it was apparent that he was starved for companionship. The kingfish was certainly a fine catch, and he remembered that back in some year or other his father had caught one which scaled at ninety-five pounds.

After lunch Bony was introduced to further treasures and was genuinely interested in several very old maps on which only parts of Australia's west coastline were drawn, maps prepared by the old Portuguese and Dutch cartographers. Bony heard the car leave for Timbertown and following afternoon tea served by Mrs Rhudder, he made his excuses.

The morning certainly had been exciting and the afternoon full of absorbing interest. He left old Jeff no longer being difficult, and felt that Mrs Rhudder was well satisfied with his efforts in cheering her husband.

Driving back to the Jukes he was able to employ his mind wholly on Sadie Stark. Like all Mona Lisas she wasn't so deep once a man awoke to her peculiar personality. It is the mysticism which attracts the white man, making of him a fly caught in the web of magnetic eyes and a slow smile. Such female power would have no influence over an aborigine, and Bony was half-way to the aborigine.

Was there any significance in there being only one tea mug? Was the delay in warning him of the sneaker intended? Had the sneaker won there would, of course, have been no use for a second mug. And then, as it turned out, had the confidences about Marvin been intended to confirm the story that Marvin had left the district?

When the wise man doesn't fall for a Mona Lisa, then he must respect her. Bony had respected this local one from the moment she had studied him obliquely under the pressure lamp in Matt's living-room.

Chapter Sixteen

Takes a Woman to Know a Woman

Scrabbling up a rock with a sneaker after you in the morning, and riding a black gelding full of steam in the afternoon are not common occupational risks for normal detectives. Even the over-imaginative could not envisage a representative of either the F.B.I, or Scotland Yard being thus employed when on duty.

The gelding needed exercise, and he had certainly been exercised when he and his rider reached the camp back of the ridge. Neck-roped to a tree, he was deflated, and an ugly memory was almost expunged from Bony's current thoughts.

Constable Tom Breckoff came down to meet him.

"Bored yet to the point of mutiny?" asked Bony, making for shade and there producing the inevitable tobacco and papers.

"Quite a vacation, Nat. You caught a good fish."

"A forty-pound kingey. Oh, I was forgetting. I brought a few pounds of cutlets, and Emma sent a tin of lard. Here, put it somewhere away from the flies."

Breckoff looked his gratitude when taking the fish to the fly-proof safe suspended from a branch.

"I was never lucky enough to get one that big. Trust those Rhudders to know the best places. We saw you bring it over the sand-bar to your car. We watched you take it to the homestead meat-house. And I won a bet of a couple of bob off Lew who said you'd forget us. Hey, Lew! You owe me two bob."

Lew waved and turned to look out again with Fred who had the glasses. Breckoff reported:

"Luke and Sadie went fishing late yesterday. Genuine this time. Came home with a load. Could have been for Luke to take up to Perth. Was that him left about three-thirty this morning?"

"That was he," replied Bony. "The Senior stopped him and searched his car for possum skins, and didn't find Marvin. Anything else?"

"All yesterday. This morning, though, old Jeff went on a tour of inspection. Left the house bright and early. Four-twenty ack emma. Came out at the back with what looked like a .22 rifle in his left hand and a crutch under the right armpit. Hardly light enough to shoot by. Anyway, he went in and round all the sheds, and he was still at it when Mark

Rhudder came out, and it looked as though he joined the old man on the inspection. Then Sadie came out, spoke to them for a few moments, saddled a horse and rode away after the milkers. The play ended when Mrs Rhudder came out in her dressing-gown, and she and Jeff argued for several minutes, or what looked like an argument, before the old boy went in for good and his wife had the rifle off him."

"Quite an entertainment, Tom. Now what, d'you think, was old Jeff looking for?"

"Bit hard like," replied the constable, grinning. "He could have been checking up on what Luke might have taken with him."

"It might have been that. You noted the car taking Mrs Stark and Sadie to town?"

"Yes. Sadie came out properly dressed at one-fifty-one. Got their car from the shed and picked up Mrs Stark at the yard gate at two-two."

"What were they doing in that eleven minutes?"

"The old battle-axe didn't come out right away, and the girl occupied the time filling the radiator and testing engine oil."

Bony wanted to know if the shoppers had returned and was given a negative reply. He expressed concern that the horses had been neck-roped to trees all this day following the previous day, and it was agreed that Bony would drive them back to their home paddock.

"I'm thinking of taking Lew and making a camp among that cliff tea-tree," he said. "From this point you can't see what is done on the beach either side the entrance. So I'll collect Lew late tomorrow. Clear?"

"Yes. I've been talking to the trackers about not being able to watch the beaches and the homestead at the same time. Marvin still ..."

"Is there somewhere, Tom. I think Sadie knows where he is, and from what you saw it's likely that old Jeff suspects it. Now what?"

Fred was waving to them to go up.

From the ridge Bony saw the car travelling fast beside the Inlet, and through the glasses could see the gulls rising before it and landing again after it. The evening wind was coming from the north to ruffle the water, and to the west a high-level cloud haze was about to accept the sun. Beyond the high dunes he could not see Ted's Rock, nor could he see Australia's Front Door beyond the cliff tea-trees. Mark appeared and began drafting cows into the milking shed. Eventually the car entered the rear yard and was driven directly into the car shed.

"Well, they didn't buy a case of whisky," remarked Breckoff. "Would have unloaded that at the house door."

"Could be they leave it to Mark," said Lew. "Bit heavy."

Mrs Stark came from the shed and walked across to the house. She carried a medium size wicker shopping-basket. A few moments later Sadie appeared and the watchers could see she carried nothing but her handbag. Recalling how she was dressed that morning, Bony decided she was now looking very smart in a green dress and a pink straw hat.

Half an hour later he mounted the gelding and drove the horses back to the homestead yards for Matt to say what paddock they should be put into. It was then after six, and, at dinner, he opened the subject of sneakers.

"The one which came this morning wasn't at all like the one we saw coming in round the Door. The sea was flat, and the first I saw of it it looked like an oil slick."

"I told you, didn't I, that when the sea's flat that's the time a sneaker is most dangerous?" responded Matt.

"How far out do the liners pass, steaming east?"

"About four miles," Matt answered. "Where did you fish?"

"Off that big rock beyond the sand-dunes," Bony replied, diffidently.

"Ted's Rock. He was taken off that rock. On a day like this, at low tide, it often happens a sneaker comes in fast and it's rising up under you when you expect it to rise high and break before hitting the rock. Sadie was watching, eh?"

The question was almost idly put and required no answer. Bony merely nodded and continued to enjoy the thick fish cutlet done in eggs and breadcrumbs to a crisp brown.

"You get big kingeys at times off that rock," Karl said, and told of catches in the past, and after a period Bony spoke again to Matt.

"Would I be right in saying that after first sighting a sneaker under today's conditions it would take only twenty seconds to reach the rock?"

"It wouldn't be any more."

Emma changed the subject by asking if he had had a nice lunch at the Inlet, and he occupied five to ten minutes speaking of his reception by old Jeff and his wife before asking if Sadie and her mother had called in.

"Sadie came in to ask if we wanted anything in town," replied Emma. "It happened that I did want some dish-towels, and a kettle for the primus. She brought the things back."

"Did Sadie say what they were going to buy in town?"

"Yes, that she was going to buy herself a couple of house frocks."

"Summery, gay, light kind of dresses, eh?"

"Oh yes. There's some pretty dresses to be got nowadays."

"When she came in on the way back with your things did she say she had bought the dresses?"

"She did. My! What a man you are, Nat," Emma chided him, her eyes twinkling. "So interested in women's clothes."

"Well, I was wondering what they went for. Tell me this. Let us suppose I took you to town, and you bought a nice dress, they'd pack it in a bundle at the store?"

"No, of course, they wouldn't. You get it in a flat cardboard box."

"Good! Now, when I brought you home and ran the car straight into the motor-shed, and you got out and walked to the house, would you leave the box with the dress back in the car, or would you want to bring it with you to look at the first available moment?"

"She wouldn't leave it in the car," interposed Matt emphatically. "Emma wouldn't leave anything in the car."

"Well, I wouldn't forget and leave a dress."

"Perhaps Sadie didn't buy a dress today," persisted Bony.

"But she said she did. I asked her if she'd got what she wanted and she told me she had."

"Then it could be that Sadie is a little liar. I wonder if we could check that. How many stores are there in Timbertown?"

"Only one where Sadie would stop for a house-frock. Is it important?"

"It could be important to know if Sadie told the truth or not. It would be important if we found that Sadie told a lie about so trivial a thing as a house-frock. She could be expected to lie if she bought, say, clothes for Marvin. Even so, why mention a house-frock at all? I must check for several reasons. From the ridge I could see her walking from the shed to the house without carrying anything except her handbag, and her mother had a small shopping-basket. You say the store people wouldn't wrap the dress into a small rolled up parcel which could have been in Mrs Stark's basket. If Sadie had bought the frock, then why didn't she carry it to the house to open the box and admire her purchase as a normal woman would do? I waited for more than half an hour, and even then she didn't return to the car for the box."

"I'll tell you what, Nat," Emma said brightly. "We've never caught out Sadie telling a lie, have we, Matt? I have a good friend who manages the dress section at Baumont's. She'd tell me what Sadie bought."

"Too late now, and Muriel's not on the phone," Matt objected.

"Then I'll take Emma to talk with this friend tonight."

"That will be nice, Nat," Emma said, and Matt chimed in:

"All right, when do we start?"

"You don't start, Matt. You stay at home and hold the fort. Emma, please get ready. We'll do most of the trip to town in daylight."

Emma looked doubtfully at Matt, and Matt nodded assent and was supported by Karl.

"Do you good, Missus. After we cleaned up, Matt can read the blood-and-gutzer for a change. He's been having it a bit too easy."

Emma and Bony left thirty minutes later, and he surprised her by stopping the car and switching off the ignition, and then getting out and standing to one side. Until a small bird flew from one stately tree to another, nothing moved in this part of the forest. The level field of bracken, the taller fronds of the tree-ferns, the silver and brown trunks of the great trees raising high their canopies of leaves to trap the light of the sunset sky, all were as stilled as though caught by a camera. Until a wattle-bird chortled it was utterly silent.

"If only all Australia was like this forest," Bony said when driving again. "So cool and silent and waiting, as it has been waiting for a million years and won't mind waiting for another million. Waiting for what? Sadie? Dress Sadie in close-fitting moss-green clothes, give her a green felt hat to wear, have her sit on the top of a fern-tree, and you'd see one of the Little People who might tell you what the forest is waiting for. Sadie of the mysterious smile, of the all-knowing, pitying eyes, Sadie who has lived for a million years."

Following a short silence, Emma said:

"You're a strange man, Nat. You've made me see Sadie for the first time, and we've known her for twenty-five years."

"You know, Emma, there have been occasions when I wished I had my Marie with me. Marie isn't at all like Sadie. Marie is stout and comfortable with my arm about her, and when I kiss an earlobe or pat her well-padded behind she gurgles, and the laughter is a light in her black eyes. To her everyone is as a printed page. She can read me as easily as a book. She could read Sadie aloud for me."

"Then she's pretty good at reading if she can read you, Nat. Marie is your wife, I think you said."

"Marie is my sweetheart and my wife, the mother of my sons and my mother. She is both my master and my slave. And to be all that she hasn't to be a Mona Lisa."

"Do you dislike Sadie?"

"Certainly I do not. What I am trying to say is that to my Marie, Sadie would be no problem. I won't admit to you that she's a problem to me. But ..."

Emma continued to relax in the car, and was content with her thoughts. She was feeling that her own life was as limited as one of her broody hens, and that the man beside her was an eagle temporarily interested in a mislaid egg. It was dark when they reached town and she directed the driver to stop at one of the neat timber-built houses.

Having witnessed Emma being welcomed by her friend, Bony smoked a cigarette and was about to toss the butt to the roadway, and thereby commit a felony in this fire-endangered area, when a gruff voice said:

"Could cost you a quid, or three months."

"Hullo, Sam! Get in before you book me for thinking of other matters."

The large, raw-boned policeman slid into the car. "Business or a spree?"

"Business."

"Oh! I was hoping it was a spree. I got a couple of bottles at home in the fridge."

"The spree shall follow the business," Bony said, lightly. "Did you see the Stark women in town this afternoon?"

"It's my town, isn't it? I saw both of them. The old lady spent the afternoon at a friend's place, and young Sadie did some shopping."

"Where did she shop? What did she buy?"

"At Baumont's Store. Came out with a few things in a basket, and one of the girls brought out a longish and flattish parcel, and another one what looked like a shoe-box. Good news!"

"Where were they stowed, the parcels?"

"In the boot. Sadie said she wanted them in the boot. The basket she put on the back seat. More good news?"

Chapter Seventeen

"The Plot Thickens"

Emma wasn't long with her friend, and they were able to spend an hour with Sam and his wife, the big blonde woman being vivaciously talkative and her husband tending to satisfy an excusable curiosity. They had travelled the first mile of the homeward journey in silence when Emma could restrain herself no longer.

"Don't you want to know what happened, Nat?"

"Of course. What did happen?"

"The oddest things. My friend, remember, is the manager of the millinery section of Baumont's. She didn't actually serve Sadie, but she knew just what Sadie bought this afternoon. She did buy a house-frock, a plain and cheap blue one. Then she asked to see frocks of much better quality, and she chose one of white silk having red polka dots, short puffy sleeves, and a frilly skirt. She said she wanted it for a young girlfriend. It was a pretty dress and expensive.

"The assistant was about to put the house-frock in with the white dress when Sadie told her not to as the dress was for her friend and the house-frock could be folded into an ordinary parcel. Then she went to the shoe department where she bought a pair of red strapped shoes."

"So she didn't lie when she said she'd bought a house-frock?" Bony commented.

"No, that was true. Sadie wanted a hat, and she was difficult about the hat and didn't buy one after all. She bought a pair of long cotton gloves, white ones. And a large bottle of boronia. Now what's funny about all this, Nat, is that Sadie paid for everything with cash, when for years everything she and her mother have bought at Baumont's has been put on the Rhudder account. Of course, being a present for a friend, Sadie mightn't have wanted it charged to old Jeff."

"That's understandable, Emma," Bony said. "Has she many friends?"

"Many friends! No, Nat."

"Then the white dress with the polka dots could be intended for herself. She might have the idea of surprising her mother and Mrs Rhudder by wearing it at a party or social engagement."

"Not that dress, Nat. Sadie's much too old for it. It's a dress for a girl of seventeen. No, it wouldn't be for herself. My friend is sure of that. There's something else, too."

Emma waited for encouragement, and being prompted, said:

"An ordinary young girl of about seventeen doesn't wear a size six shoe. Sadie does, so the shoes must be for herself, and she said the shoes were to go with the dress. She wouldn't be going screwy, would she?"

"No, I don't think she's unbalanced, Emma. And you don't, either. It's turned out to be a nice little mystery, hasn't it? One with an easy solution, probably. I like your friend Elsie Sasoon. She seemed very happy to see us."

"Else is always happy to have people call in," Emma agreed. "They've always been good friends to us. We like them immensely. Sam's easy going, but he's a good policeman."

Bony related the incident of the cigarette-butt, and Emma said:

"He'd have booked you if you had tossed the butt to the street. And laughed and laughed for weeks after. Are you pleased with what I found out?"

"Yes, of course. It does prove that Sadie isn't a liar, and I am glad about that. Is boronia her favourite perfume?"

"Always been her favourite. I don't remember her wearing anything but."

The headlights picked out the well-defined dusty road and made of the world ahead a vast cathedral crowded with white pillars supporting a roof blackened by the ages. Bony expected moonlight and thought of the western cloud-haze which now must thwart the moon.

"Old Jeff was annoyed yesterday about two candlesticks which neither his wife nor Sadie nor Mrs Stark remembered last seeing. They were of iron and very old, and he told me his grandfather discovered them in an old chest he'd found in a cave, and which must have been taken there by a shipwrecked crew. Never mind why a shipwrecked crew would take them to a cave."

"I think I've seen them but don't know when," Emma said, having to be removed from the subject of clothes and fashions. "Heavy things that couldn't be knocked over and cause a fire. Wait a minute! One of them they used as a doorstop. Jeff must be getting touchy."

"Anyway, he's missed them, and it was the basis of his being difficult, as Mrs Rhudder told you. How did he get along with Luke, d'you know?"

"Never much, Nat. In the beginning it was always Marvin with them both. Luke probably resented having to take second place, but he was always friends with Marvin. When he went away to Perth he was sort of off the scene, and what love they had had for Marvin was given to Mark, who stayed and worked. We don't know what they'd have done without Mark."

"And Sadie?"

"Well, Sadie's always been an outdoor girl. She does as much almost as a hired hand, what with doctoring the cattle and looking after the calves, and the sheep."

"A reserved type, Mark," mused Bony, braking sharply to avoid a wallaby which flashed across the road. "Says little but thinks a lot. Is he interested in girls, love affairs, usual interests of his age group?"

"I did hear he's interested in a girl in Manjimup, but how serious no one seems to know. As you said, he's the quiet type. Never says much, and when he asks a question you feel you're being caught out in a lie. It was all so different in the old days."

"You mean years ago?"

"I mean before Marvin almost murdered our Rose." Emma gently touched Bony's hand on the wheel. "You've been nice and thoughtful about that, Nat. But when you have to talk about that time, just do it without thinking to hurt. We've lived so close to it, Matt and me, and talking about it often, brings it out like, and wouldn't do us any harm. Why, Matt's become a different man since you came."

"Less bitter?"

"No, not less bitter. Less bottled up. Not anywhere near as touchy."

"I'm glad to hear it. Let's go back to Luke. Shortly after Marvin returned home they sent for Luke to handle him." Emma exclaimed, and swiftly Bony stopped the question, saying: "That wallaby told me about it when he jumped across the road. When I said they sent for Luke, I'm not including old Jeff, because I believe that the 'they' kept it from him. The reason for my subtle questions, Emma, is that I want the answer to a climactic one which is: When old Jeff was poking about the outhouses very early yesterday morning, and had a rifle with him, was he looking for the candlesticks because he thought Luke had taken them back to Perth or because he thought they had been given to Marvin to illuminate his dark hideaway, strongly suspecting that Marvin had come home and he was being kept in ignorance of it?"

"I hardly know how to answer, Nat," Emma replied after much pondering. "Matt would answer that better than me."

"There are questions which a woman can answer much more logically than a man," Bony said. "And, too, I can stop you asking me more and more questions, when Matt would brood when rebuffed. So we don't mention this little conversation to him, do we?"

"Not if you want it like that."

"Good! Afterwards, after it's all over and done with, then we need withhold nothing from him. Now what of my question? I'll put it to you again."

Again Emma took time to think, before saying:

"Old Jeff is very possessive, especially of his treasures. The candlesticks were old, and heavy, and in my opinion good enough only for door-stops. Jeff might think different. I don't know if they'd be worth anything. They could be, and Luke could have taken them. He and his wife aren't well off. You said Jeff had a rifle. No, I don't think he'd be looking for Marvin so much as for his treasures."

Following another pause, Emma said:

"We knew a man years ago who had a silly sort of wife. She'd get out of bed in the night and go and stand in the creek and threaten to drown herself. In the end the husband got tired of it, and one night when he found her in the creek with water to her knees, he told her to get on with the drowning, and went back to bed, and in ten minutes she was back in bed, too. And never did it again. Old Jeff's been threatening to shoot Marvin for years and years, and I'm quite sure he never would. It's the deep thinkers who threaten this and that, and never do it."

Bony laughed, and said:

"You're something of a deep thinker yourself, Emma. Where did you study your psychology?"

"Study it! Why nowhere. Oh, I see what you mean, Nat. Read it all in Karl's blood-and-gutzers. I've read hundreds to him. The woman in the creek, though, was real."

The Jukes's mail-box nailed to a jarrah-tree showed in their lights, and Bony slowed to take the turn-off, and parked his car for the night outside the gate in the picket-fence. Matt had been told by the dogs of their coming, and had coffee made. Emma related all her discoveries in Timbertown and Matt could make nothing of it, and said so, and why all her excitement! However, the fact that Sadie had paid for her purchases instead of having the articles debited to the Rhudder account did make him think.

Afterwards, Bony asked to look into their family album, and again he handled it with obvious care. Turning over the pages, glancing at this and that picture, he came close to the end of the record when he stopped to study a particular group. The picture presented, from the left, Marvin, Sadie, Rose and Ted Jukes. The two boys were in cricket flannels and wearing caps having club colours. Marvin had pads on and was negligently holding a bat, as though ready to be called to the wicket. Sadie and Rose wore summer frocks, and that worn by Sadie was white with polka dots and a frilly skirt, the polka dots coming out black.

It was a happy picture, a record of a happy group. Ted Jukes was laughing and holding his right hand in a gesture of pretended mockery, and remembering what Emma had said, without diffidence he placed the album before Matt.

"Do you remember when that was taken?" he asked. Matt looked at the picture and unhesitatingly replied.

"Yes. It was taken on Marvin's last holidays from College. It was at the match with Timbertown. Ted knocked up forty-one that time, and beat Marvin who only scored ten. For once our Ted did better than Marvin."

Emma, unable to restrain her curiosity, left her chair and looked over Matt's shoulder. A faint gasp left her, and Matt asked what was wrong.

"I remember now," she said, looking at Bony, admiringly. "I can see all of them as they were that day. Sadie was wearing a white dress with red polka dots. It must be just over fourteen years now. And the dress she got today would be just like the dress she wore then. What on earth is the girl about?"

Matt's strong and stubby ringers were threatening the edge of the thick page, and gently Bony drew the album from him, closed it and gave it back to Emma, who returned it to the desk drawer. On coming back to the table, she found her husband staring up at the lamp without seeing it, and Bony slowly rolling a cigarette.

An absurd cliché knocked and knocked against his mind like a bird wanting to enter a room. The plot thickens, the plot thickens. To stop it rather than develop an argument, he said:

"With her mother she goes to Timbertown, ostensibly to purchase a house-gown, which she does. While her mother is visiting a friend she makes a number of purchases for herself which she pays for with cash instead of having the goods put on the Rhudder account. On leaving the store, the items bought for you, Emma, the house-gown and a few oddments in the basket she put into the car, and the white dress and shoes go into the boot. On getting home the mother takes the shopping-basket to the house, and Sadie leaves the dress and the shoes in the boot. Half an hour later they are still in the boot. Sadie didn't hurry back from the house to get them.

"Question. Did she purchase the dress and the shoes and gloves without her mother knowing anything of it? Question. Did she make the purchases to present to a young girl-friend, as she told the sales girl, or did she buy them for herself? If for herself, why? Question. What the devil is it all about?"

Chapter Eighteen

The First Break

After breakfast the next morning Bony drove to the ridge with bread and meat and additional supplies. The morning was overcast, the sun coming through the high cloud as a disc of dull white, too anaemic to burn the haze from the sky. The wind came from the east, dry and hot and weak.

Fred was on duty with the glasses, and just below him Lew lay on his back with his hat covering his eyes. Constable Breckoff, wearing blue pyjamas, staggered from the tent blinking sleep from his eyes and looking guilty. The guilt was vanquished by eagerness. He said with undisguised enthusiasm:

"Doings last night, Nat. Things are looking up. Hey, Lew! Come on down and put this stuff away. Lew'll fix it, Nat. Come on up to the ridge. Something to show you."

Without bothering with boots or slippers, Breckoff climbed the slope ahead of Bony, and when with Fred, the constable said:

"Take a sight from this stick to that one there, and I'll tell you. I was on the job. It was a dark night, no moon. I could see as usual the Leeuwin Light doing its work. I saw the lights of a liner coming from Albany way, and just before she got off the Inlet entrance, someone in those tea-trees used a torch. Take a sighting. I jammed those sticks in to make the position sure."

Bony brought the two sticks into line with his eyes, and he found himself concentrating on the place where Matt and he had talked and the unknown man had tried to overhear their conversation. That was at the top of the rough way up from behind Australia's Front Door.

Turning over from lying on his chest, he sat up and automatically produced cigarette papers and tobacco.

"What time?" he asked, interest well suppressed.

"Two-nineteen. First the light came obliquely in flashes as though just to show the way. Then it came direct to me, being brighter than a star. After that it didn't show again. Someone came up from the beach there, I'll bet on it."

"Must be optimistic, having won two bob yesterday," Bony said, lighting the cigarette and carefully prodding the burned match into the sandy soil. "The person could have been coming out of a tea-tree clump or from the far side of one. Anyway, you saw the torch beam when still able to see the ship's lights?"

"Correct."

"You did not subsequently see a ship passing the other way?"

"No. There was only the one ship. Besides, her lights were less bright than the torch when aimed straight this way." Satisfied, Bony permitted interest in his voice.

"You have maintained a night-watch since being here?"

"Yes, of course. It's why you found me in the bunk."

"I shall remember you in my report. After I left yesterday, did Sadie return to their car for a parcel, anything?"

"No. She came out of the house by the back at six-thirty-five and went across to the yards where there were some calves. Then she went to an outhouse, and back again to the calves with what looked like a small tin."

"Giving a calf a drench, most like," interposed Fred. "After that she was in the garden with Mrs Rhudder until it got too dark for us to make out anything. Even the moon didn't help," concluded Breckoff, and smothered a yawn.

"You go back to bed, Tom, otherwise you'll be no good tonight, and you seem to be pretty good at night. Away you go. By the way, on the car seat are some letters for you."

"Thanks, Ins ... Nat. I can do with a slumber." The dark eyes in the square face became appealing. "Are we getting warm, d'you think?"

"There's a promise of a roasting in the near future," and with that Constable Tom Breckoff went down in pyjamas and bare feet to sleep with the ease of the strong.

With the glasses, Bony carefully surveyed the panoramic scene. A ship four miles and more at sea could be watched passing at night. If nearer, then only when passing off the sand-bar of the Inlet. Ted's rock was hidden by the dunes, and Australia's Front Door by the tea-tree, although the latter rock was immediately opposite the ridge, and the other, with the homestead, far to the left.

The solution of one problem had brought another. From the ridge, no one could arrive at or leave, or move about the homestead without being observed, but once beyond the dunes or the cliff trees observation was no longer possible. The solution of the second problem was to mount a watch amid the tea-tree from the edge of which the beaches below were in clear view, but a watcher there would be limited in action by not knowing who might come along the cliff from the homestead. To warn a watcher stationed there from this ridge with a white cloth would mean the signal being observed also by anyone at the homestead.

"Fred," Bony said to the young aborigine, "you went to school, didn't you?" The black eyes lit with pride, and the perfect teeth were revealed by the thick lips parted in the smile.

"Too right! I got my Leaving Certificate at home."

"Then tell me this. If I were camped over in the cliff scrub, and didn't want to come out because they'd see me at the homestead, how could you tell me someone was coming my way from the house?"

"Put up a smoke?"

"No smoke, remember."

"Have a horse handy and ride like hell to tell you."

Bony shook his head, saying there would not be time for that.

"Well, you wouldn't hear if I yelled, and if I waved something them at the homestead would see me doing it. What d'you reckon?"

"Don't ask me, Fred. You went to school. It was you who won the Leaving Certificate."

Fred laughed outright, saying:

"It's like those sums we had to do. If a bloke ran round the world at ten miles an hour, how long would it take him to recover his breath. The old man would know, betcher. He's coming up now."

When Lew reached them he was breathing hard enough to have run a hundred yards, and Bony would have given him time to rest. His son, however, put the problem to him at full speed, and then said:

"Here's me backing you for a straight win, and you don't even get a place. I'm over in that scrub, see? You're here and there's Marvin coming up from the sand-bar. I can't see him. You can. How d'you tell me? Go on, Pop, use your nut."

"Smoke."

"No smoke. No nothin'. Go on, work her out. How'd grandpa do it?"

"My old man! He'd work that one. He could do anything with nothing but his sweat."

"Perhaps it could be done this way," Bony interposed as Grandpa might well be a gnawed bone of contention. "Along the ridge there are three trees. They can be seen quite distinctly from the cliff, three trees about the same distance apart, and the middle one much younger than the outside ones. Now if Marvin was coming up from the Inlet and that middle tree could be bent towards one of the others, then the fellow down on the cliff would know, wouldn't he?"

"There you are, Pop. Dead easy," mocked Fred.

"I seen those trees," sneered Lew. "How d'you make one bend towards another one? All of 'em's too tough to bend."

"But the branches can be bent," contributed Bony. "There's one sticking out parallel with the ridge and at right angles with the cliff. We obtain a length of fence-wire, attach one end to the branch and bend the branch down when Marvin is sighted. How's that?"

"Out, Nat. You've skittled the wicket," Fred said brightly. "No one at the homestead would see the wire."

"They'd see the branch bend like a train signal dropped," Lew declared. "It'd have to be done pretty slow, making out it was the wind bending that branch. Shall we try her out, Nat?"

Thus did Bony gain co-operation without high-hatting these two, and Fred offered to obtain wire from Matt's back fence. Having the wire, they examined the trees which were growing some eight feet behind and down from the summit, and selected a branch growing horizontally from the middle one. The end of the wire was fashioned to a hook, and Fred then had half an hour of exercise before succeeding in tossing it over the branch without disturbing it and so betraying human agency at work.

Bony stayed at the camp for lunch. They had a fry-pan, but as he had brought thick steaks which looked prime, he scoured the blade of the long-handled shovel, greased it slightly and cooked the meat in this fashion over the hot coals of the smokeless fire. They called Constable Breckoff to the feast, and he attended without bothering to dress. Afterwards he and Bony occupied the ridge, and the two aborigines collapsed in the shade and went to sleep.

"It was either Marvin who had that light or someone from the house returning from visiting him," Bony said, blinking his eyes and wishing he could sleep, too. "Whoever it was, needed a torch last night climbing down or up the cliff.

"I shall have to split the party. I'll take Lew and camp in that tea-tree. You will stay here with Fred. After being a forward post this will now be the base. I'll go back presently and get a ground-sheet and a blanket as we may have to spend several nights over there. Some time tonight Lew and I will hike across to an old hut where there's water, and we'll fill a tin there.

"As I pointed out to the abos, anyone in the tea-tree cannot see anyone leaving the house for the beach or cliff-top. So we devised a method whereby you can warn us and not give your position away to the Rhudders, or to Marvin who could be active in that tea-tree in daytime." Bony explained the method, concluding with:

"Pulling down the branch must be done very slowly, little by little, and when down it must be kept in that position to be sure Lew or I shall notice it. I don't think I mentioned it but there is in the main room a telescope on a pedestal. A good one. We cannot be certain that this position hasn't been detected, and a watch on us maintained. They could have noted sunlight from the glasses, even an exposed movement up here. It's unlikely but possible.

"The objective is that neither Lew nor I is discovered, for discovery would be fatal to success. You can do nothing if you see a light at night, but that is balanced out by our ability to move about freely at night. Therefore, you get your sleep and man the post from first to last light of day. And be prepared to get an order from me to contact Sasoon for supporting action."

"That's all clear, Nat. You got a gun, I suppose?"

"I have. It's more often in my suitcase than handy for employment. I'll have a gun, you may be sure. My wife would never forgive me if Marvin shot and killed me. You know what wives are."

" 'Fraid I don't," Breckoff said, laughing.

"Doubtless you will, Tom. I'll leave you now and return in an hour or two."

Emma was laying a cloth for the afternoon tea-break when Bony walked into her living-room.

"I was planning to arrive at the psychological moment," he told her. "Where's Matt?"

"In the carpenter's shop making something, I think," Emma replied.

"Has he fixed up the siren?"

"Yes." Emma giggled. "Goes off good, too."

Stepping to the dresser she turned to look at him, and with her left hand behind her pulled open a drawer. From outside the house there came a wailing noise to be heard half a mile away. Bony smiled his satisfaction, and Emma said:

"The fire brigade'll arrive in a minute."

The brigade arrived at top speed, hatless, coatless, armed with a two-inch wood chisel. Seeing Bony, Matt wiped his forehead with a forearm, grinned, sat down.

"I didn't hear you come back, Nat," he said sheepishly, and then laughed. "Works all right, doesn't it?"

"Yes, but don't go too far from the house," Bony urged. "I've got news for you that will make you more cautious, both of you."

He told them about the mystery light, and added: "It's the first plain intimation that Marvin is still down there, and I'm taking Lew with me to flush him out. Go on, Emma, pour the tea. Later I'll want you to find for me a ground-sheet and a blanket, and tucker and a petrol-tin for water. Now for Sasoon."

Sasoon wasn't in his office, and presently Elsie answered the call to say he was out somewhere with the other constable, and would he ring back?

"Doesn't matter, Elsie. A message will do. You have pad and pencil handy?" He knew that Matt and Emma were silent and expectant, and chose the moment to impress them further of the seriousness of the situation, should Marvin Rhudder ever break this way. "Right. Take this, Elsie, please. 'Hold yourself for instant action. Take the telephone to bed with you.' Yes, that's all, Elsie, and thank you. Thanks, too, for the supper last night. Emma! Oh, all right, all right! I'll tell her you want to gossip non-stop."

Chapter Nineteen

The Secret Cave

The sun was huge and lustreless, a red sphere which sank into the Indian Ocean beyond the Leeuwin Light. While one counted ten, the sky at zenith above the ridge to the graveyard of the sun was a soiled pink drape, becoming as the wrapping of a five-thousand-year-old mummy before night came to obliterate the obscenity.

"Smoke from bush fires," was Bony's opinion.

"Storm," commented Lew, the Wise Man behind Australia's Front Door.

They manned the post on the ridge, and in the dell below, Constable Thomas Breckoff was wondering anxiously how to thicken a fish stew. With him was Fred who had advised mashing the potatoes and adding the mash to the bubbling stew in the large billycan. Away at the homestead, Sadie Stark was taking the herd of milkers to the night pastures, and Mark Rhudder was carrying pails of skimmed milk to feed the yarded calves. Pale smoke was rising from a chimney and drifting across the Inlet, and Mrs Rhudder was pottering about her garden. The gulls dotted the shores of the quiet water, and from the ocean came the beat and slap of the eternal surges.

The stew turned out to be quite good, with the addition of a little pepper and a shake or two of salt. In the light of the fire they ate with relish, and Breckoff additionally with pride. In the calm and cool of the night they went up again to the lookout, there to talk and take care to shield the strike of a match. Other than a point of dull light at the homestead and the faraway slashes of the lighthouse against the sky, the world was painted out with black.

For something better to occupy time, Bony brought up the subject of Marvin Rhudder, and his early years, and reaped a moderate harvest.

"Were you at a cricket match in Timbertown just before Marvin Rhudder left that last time?"

"Too right," promptly replied Fred. "I don't ever forget that game. Marvin tried to kill me. Remember, Pop?"

"Ought to, as I was umpiring for the Inlet United. The Timber Fallers beat the Inlet that time. Could of been what upset Marvin."

"He was always upset, even in them days, Pop. You know that. He was the meanest bastard what ever lived." Fred fell silent, and it was

Breckoff who spurred him. "Well, the Inlet United came up to play the Timber Fallers. I was working in town then, and I played against the Inlet. As usual when he was home, Marvin was captain of the Inlet, and he won the toss against the Fallers and said they'd bat first.

"Marvin sent in Ted Jukes and a bloke called Harry the Puke, because he couldn't drink without being sick, as their openers. Well, Ted Jukes got himself set, and he'd piled up thirty-odd runs when Harry was clean bowled, and Marvin put himself in as next bat. After that over, I got put on bowling for a spell, and the first one I sent down to Marvin he hit a boundary.

"Give the swine his due, Marvin was a good bat although he was always showing off. You know, taking extra time to get his block, taking more time than anyone else would do in shaping up for the strike. Everyone having to know it was the Great Marvin flashing his bat like he was Don Bradman. Twice I appealed for leg-before, and both times the verdict was against me; once by pop, here.

"Anyway, I got Ted Jukes caught out. Forty-something, it was, and a good score for Ted. And Marvin being at my end and waiting for the next batsman to come out, I said to him: 'It's going to be your push-over next.' " Fred paused to light a cigarette with a shielded match before coming to the climax of his story.

"The next ball I sent down to him he missed and I nearly got his wicket. It wasn't a hard ball, and it riled him pretty good. Then I sent him a nice easy one he could have hit for a boundary, intending to get him with my next. Well he came running up the pitch to the ball in flight, and I could see he wasn't going to hit no boundary. He drove it straight back at me with all his might. I could see the ball coming like a comet. I tried to catch it and didn't have a hope. It got me fair in the guts, and as I was waiting for the pain in the split second before it caught me I saw by his face that he'd done it on purpose, tried to and did."

"Then you was carried off the field and put into hospital," supplemented Lew.

"Nice bloke," Breckoff interposed.

"When I got out of hospital he was out of the picture," Fred said, sadly. "One thing about Marvin was that he couldn't fight. I could use myself, couldn't I, pop?"

"Too true," agreed Pop, and retired into silence.

"How did he get on with the girls?" asked Bony.

"You mean Rose Jukes and Sadie Stark? Treated 'em like dirt, like he treated all the others in Timbertown. They liked it, too. You could see 'em wanting to grovel like a thrashed pup. White or black, they all went for

Marvin like he was a film groaner."

"Including Rose and Sadie?"

"Including them, it seemed like to me," answered Fred. "Course they was raised with Marvin and a bit more used to him. But the others!"

Bony couldn't see the shrug which must have followed, and he pondered the question of taking young Fred with him in preference to the far more experienced bushman his father would be. Lew and Fred gave other pictures of Marvin Rhudder, or rather pictures of him from different angles. He had never been a hero to these aborigines, and probably had never tried to suppress in their presence those facets of his character he had so successfully hidden from white people, including the mental specialists. A Kedic! That he had ever been.

Carrying light blanket rolls and a well-filled gunny-sack Bony and Lew left camp before midnight. Not a star showed, and although the moon lightened the sky it failed to show, either. Without talking they covered the several miles to the hut by two-o'clock, and rested and smoked, and filled a four-gallon tin with water. It proved to be an awkward burden which they carried in turn.

The moon had set and the night was black. It had been decided, in view of the slight wind from the east, to reach the coast a mile westward of Australia's Front Door and the pathway down to the beach. Timing was important. They had to arrive at safe concealment before day broke and after a probable night visitor to Marvin's hideaway had returned to the homestead.

Bony chose to follow Lew who was familiar with every yard of this country, every water-gutter and empty creek carrying water to the paperbark swamp as the land inclined away from the cliff. He trod almost on Lew's heels, and never once tripped over a root or unevenness of ground, mutely acclaiming the aborigine's bush lore and eyesight. Arriving at the cliff scrub, Lew unloaded himself and whispered that they should wait for day to give its first sign.

Being the current water-carrier, Bony gladly acquiesced.

"How far are we from the cliff path behind the Door?" Bony asked when they were sitting with backs against a tree-clump, and had voted for no smoking.

"A good mile and a half. We'd better move soon's first sign of dawn, and that'll be late, replied Lew.

"You would know pretty well every cave there is, eh?"

"No fear, Nat. There's more caves and holes between here and the Leeuwin than marbles in a lottery barrel, and I seen the marbles in one once."

"Then you pick one you do know somewhere about opposite the Door, and we'll camp on the cliff above it. It must be near there that Marvin's camped."

Lew agreed, saying it would be silly to use that rough way down if Marvin's hideout was far on one side of it or the other.

"Just this side of it there's a good sort of cave me and Fred think Marvin could be usin'. Then there's another one with a water-hole in the rock what's not far from where we are now."

"We must camp close to the place where the torchlight was seen. Anyway, for a start. I'm ready to move when you say."

"Should of brought a dog. They got better smellers than us."

"I doubt that they'd have a keener nose than you, Lew. Give us plenty of time."

"All right. We could start now and slow up a bit if we're too early getting near the Door. If I swerve it'll be only to have the wind right for me smeller. That Marvin's no new chum."

They moved off, Bony allowing Lew to keep well ahead, often unable to see him and certainly never hearing him, the noise of the surf masking immediate sounds, had there been any. Presently the sky took light to itself, and against it could be seen the tops of the tree-clumps. Beside one of these Lew waited.

"Don't think so far there's anyone around," he said. "Go on?"

"Better."

Half an hour later it was possible to see the ground between the clumps, and the cliff edge silhouetted against the sea, and Bony was relieved from growing anxiety when Lew stepped from inside a clump and beckoned.

"Good enough here, Nat. Come in and stay till we can see."

What Lew meant was to get into the seclusion of the clump, and, because the interior was so dark, to remain inactive until day was strong enough to show the twisted branches and the dry debris of twigs and leaves which would create unusual noises if disturbed. The waiting period passed to show them the maze of slanting trunks and branches forming the skeleton work of the massed leaf covering, and then it was possible to select a semi-cleared space on which to make camp. This was right on the verge of the cliff.

Parting the leaf mass, Bony was able to look down at the sea almost at high tide. It was still comparatively flat, although restless even behind Australia's Front Door. To the left he made out the zigzagging path, and beyond it the overhang of rock extending for many hundreds of yards where no way down could be offered.

"There's a fair-sized cave right under us," Lew said. "Goes in a long way like a big house with plenty of rooms. Could be Marvin's camped there. There's a lot of entrances like holes to a rabbit burrow. Be a good place for him."

Bony saw now that anyone from the homestead would not pass their hidden camp to get down the beach, and further that anyone coming from the homestead could not be seen until they were on the way down at that point. He thought Lew could have chosen a better position, but decided to remain at least for a few hours. He crawled to the landward side of the clump, and was given an uninterrupted view of the ridge with its easily distinguishable trees. The signal branch was in position. Having eaten he told Lew he could sleep until noon, and Lew rested his head on his blanket roll and slept instantly. During the morning Bony alternated his attention between the beach and the ridge, and carefully removed dead timber to facilitate this divided task. He slept during the afternoon and into late evening, and Lew reported no movement. At sundown the cloud wrack thinned to permit the light of the sun to redden the Door panels, and ultimately to give the moon slight influence over the night.

All night long one of them peered over to the beach and along the cliff to the way down to it. Morning came to find the sky again painted with grey cloud and the sea as grey and leaden.

"Going to storm, all right," commented Lew, and wryly added: "Marvin's gonna be nice and dry. Us! You can wring me out and I'll wring you."

"We earn our wages the hard way, Lew. It's not raining yet, though, and if it rains real hard we'll retreat to the hut. About time something happened."

It happened about an hour after the sneaker rolled in behind Australia's Front Door. Bony was watching the tide creeping over the wide sand-flat to the rock on which he and Matt sat that first day, when Lew announced that the signal was down.

The black eyes were wide, and the mouth was drawn to part the lips and show the new white dentures in the canine's grin of anticipation. It had been a long and boring wait. The additional waiting seemed to be endless.

"What do you reckon, Lew? Come along the beach or along the cliff?" Bony asked to prevent tension.

"Cliff way. Tide's too far up to take the beach."

Despite the warning, Bony tautened his muscles and Lew emitted a faint hiss when abruptly Sadie stood on the cliff above the path. She was wearing old clothes as when supposedly watching for Bony. Hatless, her hair seemed to take a tinge of blueness from the sky. For a few moments she stood there as though calculating the risks of the beach, and then moved the gunny-sack strap to her neck the better to use both hands in the descent. The sack was bulky.

"Taking him grub and water," whispered Lew. "Must be water. None in the caves below."

Sadie progressed with great care as though the contents of the bag were both precious and fragile, and when she had gone halfway to the pile of jumbled rocks backing the narrow beach she stopped and again regarded steadily the sea still a hundred feet below, and as steadily looked along the battlemented faces of the barrier in their direction. Lew whispered:

"Now what's she at? She's got to go all the way down and make this way to climb a bit to the caves." The hiss issued again through his teeth when Sadie neither went on down nor turned in their direction. She left the known way down and climbed over a rock out-thrust and then proceeded with apparent ease in the opposite direction towards the overhang.

"She's going away, not coming," Lew said. "No caves that way that I know, and I don't think Fred knows of one, either. We talked about this bit of cliff."

"She seems to be on a ledge," Bony observed. "Parallel with the beach."

Sadie went now with obvious confidence. She passed under the bulging rock overhang, proceeded onward for several yards, turned into the cliff face and vanished.

Chapter Twenty

The Altar

The slapping waves crept up the rock-littered beach like the cautious feet of a Tasmanian tiger. Under the unruffled surfaces of the sea could be seen the sand ripples it flowed over in its eternal surge. In the grey light Australia's Front Door, now dark and forbidding, defied the Antarctic and was indifferent to the mighty blows being prepared in the Region of Ice.

By Lew's leather-covered wrist-watch Sadie had disappeared into the rock face at one-fifty-three, and as the sun was not visible there was no other agency to check the time. Not that Bony was that interested. The minutes at first fled, then dawdled, but the tide waited not for Sadie to reappear, and eventually covered the beaches. After once again looking at his watch. Lew said:

"Nearly twenty to four. Must be spending all the afternoon with Marvin."

At ten minutes to five, Lew said with impatience strange in an aborigine:

"Could be another way up."

"Unlikely there is another way to the top less difficult than the one she came down by, Lew. Take it easy. She's having a good old gossip with Marvin. There! Look?"

Sadie Stark was again on the ledge beneath the overhang. Her gunny-sack was weightless, and now she walked almost in haste to reach the out-thrust of rock, to climb over this dangerous obstruction, and make her way up the rough pathway to the top. Then she was gone, and Lew regarded Bony with brows almost meeting, and Bony was gazing steadily at the place where Sadie had reappeared, hoping for a sign.

Marvin Rhudder did not appear, and after a long long wait and the wearing away of expectancy, Bony decided his next move.

First, he went to the rear of the clump to be assured by the tree signal that all was clear. Secondly, he ascertained the time from Lew, and tried to forecast the weather, and he gambled that the threatened storm would hold off for another twelve hours.

"He's not going to show himself in daylight, Lew. He'll come out and up to the top when it's dark, using his torch like he did the night before last. We'll shift camp closer to the place where he'll reach the top, and we'll wait for him there and knock him out, and put the cuffs on him I borrowed from Sasoon."

"Easy," agreed Lew, eyes glinting with the excitement of coming action.

"Not easy," Bony told him. "We can't play the fool with a man like Marvin. We can't just tussle with him, give him the chance of getting away into the darkness. We'll move camp right now."

They took possession of the tree-clump into which the mystery man had slipped, and at once Bony stationed himself at the edge of the cliff and within two yards of the point where Sadie had gained the top. Lew was looking around for a suitable length of wood to employ as a waddy, for the plan was that as Marvin was getting to his feet at the cliff Bony was to tackle him about the legs and Lew was to lay him out.

Here they were stationed in the clear between the tea-tree where the ridge and its signal-tree could be seen until it grew dark. Their rear, therefore, was maintained as the signal did not fall to danger. The sea left the beaches and drained away over the sand-flats, and vanished. The Front Door of Australia loomed like the back of a guarding giant until the night shrouded it.

"Don't you hit too hard," Bony softly urged Lew. "We want him on the gallows-trap, remember. And don't miss, although it's an insult to tell you about that. Now, no more talking."

The night hours passed by in racking progression, and there was no evidence that the animal had left its lair. The new day, drab and sickly, found Lew asleep and Bony decided on his next move. As Marvin hadn't come up to be clubbed and captured, he would go down before Marvin could be expected to waken. There would be unavoidable risks, but then there would be risks in any set of circumstances applicable to this present situation.

The wiser course would be to send Lew for reinforcements armed with rifles, to block off this section of cliff and either starve or thirst the hunted man into surrender. That would be the routine plan to adopt, and it was a hundred to one it would never succeed in this terrain and governed by the ruling conditions.

Only a fool would think that Marvin Rhudder would surrender tamely; that he was unarmed; that he lacked the intelligence to take evasive action; that he was ignorant of the cracks and crevices, the caves and caverns comprising every hundred yards of this part of the coast. And did Marvin break his neck on the rocks, or should he be drowned, when seeking to escape arrest, no credit would be given Inspector Bonaparte.

Rousing the aborigine, they ate and drank sparingly of the water. Then Lew was taken several yards along the cliff and shown a heavy boulder which could be pushed over in the event that the ridge signalled approach from the rear. He was given clearly to understand that if Bony had not returned by noon he was to report to Breckoff and bring assistance. Thus it was hoped that the boulder would give the alarm by its crashing.

Once over the cliff edge Bony went down with care not to dislodge a rock-splinter or one of the large pebbles which might start an avalanche. He carried an automatic in his right hand and from his hip pocket protruded the bulb end of a powerful torch. The handcuffs he left with Lew to bring down when needed, and he was coldly determined to shoot Rhudder in a leg at the slightest excuse given him. He was not burdened with illusions of acting fairly to this insult to the human race.

Poor Marvin Rhudder! Poor sick Marvin! Marvin Rhudder so needful of tact and understanding. The poor man, always hunted by the police, always hounded into court and then into prison, as they hounded those poor desperate convicts sent out from England only because they stole a rabbit to save themselves from starving to death. Vote for the Government that won't hang! Vote for the Mercy Party!

And yet he was another policeman doing his job to help preserve the peace and protect people from violence, from degenerates and killers.

On coming to the place where Sadie had left the descending path, he saw that the out-thrust of rock concealed the ledge running away parallel with the beach, and thus Lew was given full marks for knowing of the place ahead into which Sadie had gone. Here, too, he employed care because a slip could mean a broken limb, and on the far side found an uneven ledge of varying width. At places the wind-driven sand lay deep and here were Sadie's footprints.

He glanced upward for a sight of Lew, and remembering the heavy boulder, hoped the aborigine would think to look first before he had to roll it over. All he did see was a black hand being waved to him.

Pressing on he came under the bulging rock overhang, following the ledge which now was a mere eighteen inches, wide, until he came to a shoulder of the rock wall. Here he stopped. Here he gave himself a full minute to recover from the rush descent, and to strain his hearing to detect human sounds above the noises of the sea. Breathing returned to normal, muscles rested, and nerves calmed by the fixation of the mind upon one purpose, he edged round the shoulder, to see cliff-face beyond face, surmounted by the fringe of scrub and based upon the jumble of rocks termed beaches. Ten yards distant a black orifice in the dark-grey wall indicated a cave.

Without haste he covered those ten yards to bring his back to the wall outside the hole. It was higher than he and five feet wide. Again he listened for human proximity, heard nothing to betray a sleeper, or human movement. Slowly he moved forward, round and into the entrance of what he came to see was a very deep cavern for there was no light from its interior. He was astonished by the hurricane lamp on the ledge of rock some four feet inside what was the passage-like entrance. Maintaining his back against the rock wall, he worked into the entrance till opposite the lamp. Beside it was a tin box obviously containing wax matches.

He halted here, regarding the lamp and the matchbox whilst his startled mind recovered from the slight shock of seeing these ordinary mundane objects. His left ear subconsciously sought human sounds, his right registered the little noises of the sea which came creeping in after him. With them came the air current to defeat his nose.

The lamp reflected the daylight as dull pewter. It was of the cheap but efficient kind found on every farm. Both it and the match-box were untarnished by the salt air, and appeared to be placed there for use by a visitor. Aware that he was exposed against the light to anyone deep in the cavern, he moved on again eventually to come to another corner and find on its far side safety in the darkness.

Here he could register smells, or rather only one smell which triumphed over others, the perfume of boronia strong and pervading. He was unsure that he could detect the smell of kerosene, and there seemed to be another smell he could not name. The interior silence emphasized the exterior noises. With his feet he found stones, and picking one up he tossed it from him. It fell with a soft thud. Sandy floor. He tossed another and this one clunked on rock. Falling to his knees he tossed more stones in varying directions, and then bending forward to bring himself nearer the floor, he called:

"Come forward with your hands up, Marvin Rhudder. Police here. Quite a bunch outside, waiting to take you."

No one answered, there was not even the echo of his own voice.

Having announced his presence, Bony was aware that all the advantages lay with Marvin. Marvin had merely to sit and wait. He knew every twist and turn of this place, every obstruction. Time was on his side in any battle of nerves, and such a contest must not be permitted. Bony straightened his arm to one side and flashed on the torch.

The brilliant beam sliced the darkness to contact dark rock. There was no shot. The beam moved to one side, crept along the rock wall, came to an opening, hesitated in order to probe, moved on again. Still no shot, and in Bony growing confidence that the place was not inhabited. His light illumined a pressure lamp hung from a peg driven into the wall. A metallic gleam came from below the lamp, and the torch revealed a large box or chest with heavy brass bolt and socket.

In Bony's hand the light disc went back and round the wall to his left, and there came into view a box-shaped rock lying on a sand foundation and clear of the wall. On this rock were two heavy candlesticks in which remained the butts of white candles. Between them lay what appeared to be a beret. From it there returned to Bony the reflection of a silver cross within a circle.

Bony advanced to this rock and almost tripped on the rocky floor. His light revealed the floor to be ribbed by rock, the ribs separated by swathes of fine sand, dry and soft. The sand was much disturbed by human feet, and the impressions greatly blurred. Coming to the isolated rock, the first oddity of several was that the sand on which it rested bore no imprints, was as smooth as though worked on by the thin edge of a board.

The rock itself was about three feet high, eight feet long, and some three feet wide, The top was level, almost flat. The candlesticks were eighteen inches high, each having a square base so that a hard blow would be necessary to upset them. In the sconces the candle ends promised yet another hour of burning.

The beret! It was as an emperor's crown flanked by shoe buckles to the man who stood before it, pinning it with his light beam. The ornament proved it to be similar if not the actual beret worn by Marvin Rhudder that moonlit night he was seen by Karl Mueller. If not the actual beret it was one identically like it and described by Sasoon when he went to the Inlet on that first visit. Here it looked to be the centrepiece, with the candlesticks, of an altar.

There was lead in Bony's shoes and a lump in his stomach when he turned about and crossed to the box beneath the pressure lamp. As he had thought at first, it was a chest, a large cabin chest made of what could be mahogany, and bounded by copper hoops, with a brass bolt thrust into its keeper.

The anticlimax was affecting him as he made an examination of this cavern. He found that it extended some thirty-five feet from the tunnel-like entrance with a maximum width of about twenty feet. At the inner end several ridges of rock rose like teeth from the sandy floor, and at one side there was an opening into another and much smaller hole or cavern. The fine sand on the floor momentarily interested him, and the only explanation for its presence could be that it had been brought in by the wind, or carried in by an exceptionally high tide in a past age.

Coming again to the entrance he stood there to smoke a cigarette and sternly readjust his mind following the period of great tension. It was now obvious that the man he sought was no longer living in this place, if ever he had lived in it. His beret was here, and his suitcase with personal articles, and the money for which, with little doubt, he had murdered, had been hidden in a hollow tree.

Sadie had told him that Marvin Rhudder had been sent away by the strong-willed Luke who himself had departed, and what he had discovered in this cavern supported the supposition that Marvin had really left many days before and that memory of him was being kept green by Sadie Stark, as parents have done by keeping on a table articles associated with a son killed in war.

Chapter Twenty-one

Record of a Knight

Had he had another assistant he could have sent him to the top to reassure Lew who would be wondering if he had been snared by Marvin Rhudder.

"Marvin wasn't down there," he said when seated with Lew. "I couldn't smell much because the place is full of Sadie's scent, boronia. Sand patches about the floor but it's too fine and dry to retain tracks."

"Then what she go down there for?" was Lew's natural question.

"I think she has taken some of Marvin's things there just to keep to herself. There's a beret much like the one he wore when he came home. There are other things which don't belong to him. I saw a big copper-bound chest, a couple of old candlesticks, three old-time harpoons and a broken-handled shovel. Then in a smaller cave off the big one, I came on a kerosene box in which there were knives and forks and spoons, tin pannikins and plates, everything rusty and not used for years. Another examination of the place will probably reveal other articles."

"Harpoons!" said Lew. "Why harpoons down there?"

"I think it could be this way. Long before Marvin left home for good, he and the other boys and the two girls made that cavern their secret camping place. It must have been after your son fell out with them, otherwise he would have told you about it. On a ledge there was a cigar-box containing fish-hooks and lead sinkers, and they looked old and rusty."

"See in the chest, Nat?"

"I didn't look. I'm saving that till next time. And I want to be down there when Sadie calls next time, too."

Having mentally digested this information, Lew said that Marvin 'must be someplace else', and Bony told him of his conviction that Marvin had left this part of Australia.

"Then we can go home, eh? We're getting short of tucker."

"If you had gone to school like Fred, Lew, you'd know that the word conviction isn't another word for proof. We have to have the proof, and when Sadie comes next time, she'll give us the proof by what she does down in that cavern. What do you think she does down there all the afternoon?"

"Ask me another, Nat." The aborigine grinned mirthfully. "Me, I'm only an old abo what never went to school like Fred. What about look-seeing into that cave I told you about under our last camp?"

"All right. I'll keep watch up here."

"Might run into Marvin in that cave," Lew said, gravely.

"You'd be lucky, Lew. Ask him up for a drink of water and the last of our tucker."

"No fear. You can have that Marvin feller. He's not copping me from behind a rock."

"You'd sooner go home?"

"Dunno." Lew grinned his cheerful grin. "Might be better here starvin' than be home workin'." He thinned his voice to a high whine. "Get away from me, Lew. Now where you been and the dinner waiting an' all. An' me cooking with no wood in the stove. An' no tobaccer 'cos you pinched it all."

"Home can't be that bad, Lew," Bony protested laughingly. This humorous interlude he found a relief after the tension and the disappointment. Lew vigorously asserted that it was worse, and that town life had ruined the women, and he became really convinced that life with Bony under conditions of starvation was preferable.

"As you won't go home, and as you won't go down to your cave to meet Marvin, then you stay right here and keep your eyes on the tree-signal while I go down and finish looking around," he was told. "And should you see the signal drop, look over before you topple this boulder because I might be under it. I won't be long."

The time by Lew's watch was shortly after ten when Bony left him, and on again entering the cavern he had decided he would use the pressure lamp as it was unlikely that Sadie would make her next visit until the afternoon, when the smell of the lamp would not be noticeable, after being extinguished.

The brilliant light changed the cavern from a place of dark menace to one approaching fairy-like beauty, and Bony made another thorough inspection of it, resulting in the discovery of a primus stove behind the chest with a tin of kerosene, and another but smaller tin containing calico bags of tea and sugar, biscuits in cellophane, a china cup, and a tin of powdered milk, half full.

Lew's eyes would have glistened at this find, for neither had drunk tea since leaving the base camp, and that now seemed days ago. He found no water, and the primus was empty of oil and appeared not to have been used for some time.

Now for the old chest which in the light of the lamp cried for cedarwood oil and the employment of sandpaper to wipe the marks of ill-usage from the wood which could be made to gleam again. Bony expected to find fishing tackle, and oddments prized by boys and girls who had adventured with blithe spirits. He raised the heavy lid and saw a white dress with red polka spots, a pair of cotton gloves and a pair of red shoes.

The lid was maintained upright by its own rear balance, and Bony gazed upon these articles with astonishment greater than when he had discovered the candlesticks. Bluebeard's umpteenth wife could not have been more surprised.

On his knees he lifted the dress carefully from the chest, keeping its folds and arrangement. With it he placed the gloves and the shoes. There was then disclosed a cuttings book, and, between several expensively-bound books, an automatic pistol of heavier calibre than his own. Aware that the use of a handkerchief would destroy rather than preserve prints, yet he used his handkerchief when taking up the weapon and sniffing at the barrel.

The perfume of boronia pervaded the cavern. Even stronger among the contents of the chest it thwarted his sense of smell, and regretting the unorthodoxy of the act, he dismantled the pistol, removing the cartridges remaining in the clip, and, finally peering through the barrel, pointed at the lamp. It was dirty, not having been cleaned after firing.

Reassembled, the pistol was laid beside the cuttings book, the cartridges now in his pocket. He removed the books from the chest, finding them to be prizes won by Marvin Rhudder when at Sunday school. There was a leather-backed folding photograph wallet and within was a studio portrait of Marvin as he must have been about the time he left home. It was a youthful face. The mouth had a quizzical smile about it. The eyes were seen here to be a shade too close together, and in them was no expression to match the mouth. Opposite this picture was one of Sadie Stark, and she was dressed in a white frock having polka dots. She was looking directly at the camera. Her eyes were wide and the expression in them was allied with the expression about her mouth and chin; the mysterious, withdrawn, all-knowing smile Bony had seen.

He found, too, what he had expected. Disjointed fishing-rods, hand-lines, a small calibre rifle, a mouth organ, old paperbacks, and a layer of oddments including sea-shells, rifle bullets, pieces of stone and rock.

Returning all the articles to the chest as near as possible to their original position, taking special care with the dress, Bony went to the entrance to smoke a cigarette and to ponder on the significance of the white frock with the polka dots, the exact replica of that worn by Sadie at the cricket match fourteen years earlier. If the dress recently purchased, and the use of boronia perfume, together with the candlesticks either side the beret was the build-up of a personality who again had departed from her life, it would mean only that Sadie was mentally abnormal. This he could not believe, despite his experience of extraordinary human behaviour.

He hadn't the exact time, but at eleven-fifteen this day Matt Jukes was studying his old barometer and thinking it must have died of age and would have to be replaced by a new one. Had Bony maintained interest in the sea instead of cogitating on his mysteries, he might have observed the phenomenon that towards the Inlet the sea for many yards outward from the beaches was a flat and unbroken expanse, and the colour tarnished copper. Had he observed this he might not have attributed it to the dismantling of the great seaweed mountain near Ted's Rock by the sea in its most passive mood.

However, he did notice that it was beginning to rain.

Passing along the passage entrance to the cavern he paused at the hurricane-lamp and match-box. It was well kept and the glass was polished. Why was the lamp there at all? Anyone familiar with this place would know of the pressure lamp which could be located in the dark. Everything was at sixes and sevens, with nothing coming out at evens.

Remembering the rain, he remembered Lew who would be feeling uncomfortable. Glancing outward he was struck by the picture of Australia's Front Door being perfectly enclosed by the frame of the passage. Had the weather been clear it would have been remarkable and memorable indeed.

Taking the cutting-books again from the chest, he closed the lid and sat on it with the book on his knees. It was spacious, and of good quality, and he lifted the front cover to see another portrait of Marvin Rhudder, and read beneath it in small and neat calligraphy:

> *He wore a Suit of Shining Mail,*
> *Evil was the Acid which Disintegrated It.*

In the centre of the next page, written by the same hand, Bony read:

> *On Monday, February 15, 1947*
> *Marvin left home to begin the Final Term*
> *At College*
> *The World waited for his Conquest*
> *And The Woman Conquered Him.*

The succeeding pages were filled with newspaper cuttings, all of them having been headline news under their dates. As Bony flicked over the pages, the following phrases and announcements reviewed a Monster's Progress.

Small Child Brutally Outraged. Man Arrested for Child Attack. Three Years for Marvin Rhudder. Woman Ravished on Allotment. Man Wanted for Rape. Marvin Rhudder Arrested for Attack on Woman. Psychiatrists Battle Over Rhudder. Rhudder Released On Bond. Couple Savaged in Park. Man Arrested for Park Crimes. Marvin Rhudder Again. Trial of Marvin Rhudder. Male Victim in Mental Hospital. Rhudder Guilty: Five Years. Rhudder Released. Public Protests. Echo of Park Crimes. Woman Walks Over Gap to Death. Royal Commission Urged.

Bony closed the book, sickened by a criminal career presented in tabloid form. Revolted, on impulse he opened it again at the last occupied page and there read:

> He Who Wore
> The Shining Suit of Mail Has Departed

So Sadie had spoken the truth. Marvin Rhudder had left the district. And somewhere there was a woman ignorant of her coming rendezvous with a human tiger. It was the end of the assignment. It would be the first time in his own career that he had failed, unless he were re-assigned at some future date, and that, he felt, would not be distant, to hunt again for Marvin Rhudder.

Replacing the cuttings-book, he reached up to turn off the pressure lamp, and then paused to survey this strange place before retreating from it to announce defeat. What a terrible set-up for a man to leave in the memory of others! The rock-like altar with the candlesticks flanking what might have been a casque worn by the man in shining mail. The care with which the altar was tended, even the sand about it smoothed and virgin.

The lamp extinguished, Bony stood for a moment listening into the darkness as though hoping to hear the echo of voices. Then he was irritated because he could not smell human beings, as he and Lew had smelled them in the hut, could not smell them for the pervading boronia perfume.

There must be another explanation for all he had seen here. Surely there was another reason than making of this place a shrine? He would wait for Sadie, wait to see what she did when next she came, wait to demand of her just when Marvin left, which way he went, and follow him even if it meant years before confronting him with a waddy and a pair of handcuffs.

The rain had thickened to blur the great rock so romantically named by a youth in shining mail. The wind was low and the sea was cold and drab and lethargic. So, too, was poor Lew.

"You been having a good time, Nat, and me as wet as a shag."

"But I didn't forget you," Bony said. "Let's get under cover. I've brought a beautiful present for you."

"What?" The rain was forgotten, and the discomfort of wet clothes. "What did you find down there?"

"Can't show it out here. Might get wet."

There were still dry places inside the arboreal igloos, but they would soon vanish did the rain continue. From inside his shirt Bony drew an old tin, and the black eyes of the aborigine gleamed when Bony lifted the lid.

"Tea," breathed Lew.

"And sugar," added Bony, producing another tin. "Make a fire. We can douse it if the signal drops. Down in that cavern where I've been there are biscuits, too. So we can eat the last of our tucker, have a drink of hot tea, and then a good hard smoke."

"Crikey! We're always having good hard smokes, Nat."

"But we can't smoke down in the cavern," Bony said, filling the billycan with the last of the water, and not worried by future lack of it.

"Why not, Nat?"

"Because you don't smoke in church, that's why not."

Chapter Twenty-two

Good Night for a Murder

As the day died in sick misery and Sadie Stark had not visited the cavern, Bony was convinced that the weather had influenced her.

They had shifted camp into the cavern, concealing their meagre equipment behind a rock upthrust at the far side, and one or other had to watch for her from the shelter of the entrance beneath the overhang. The rain had steadily increased to tropic downpour, then abruptly ceased when the light east wind changed to the north, and blew harder. For an hour it came fitfully from the west, and towards the end of the afternoon heavy swells mounted to high rollers to sweep in behind the Door and take long long bites at the shore.

On observing the great masses of weed, Lew had instantly guessed that it had once formed a mountain which the sea had disintegrated. Now they could see its slow advance along the serrated shoreline, and later on noticed how the rollers stopped it at the east side of Australia's Front Door, and began to send it back towards the Inlet. Lew said:

"Big storm coming up all right. Funny about that weed. I seen it like that before. Away to the Leeuwin it was. One day a dump of weed what'd take you half a day to walk round. Next day all the weed floating away to be built up again some other place."

"What's the coast like over by the Leeuwin?" asked Bony, for something to say.

"Good! Better'n this. Cape Leeuwin sort of protects it. Nothing like that here. Them rollers is gettin' big, ain't they?"

"I can't see them washing up and into the cavern, Lew. Must be more than a hundred feet up from the beach. How did the sand get in here? Blown in?"

"Could be. Perhaps washed in by a big sea." Lew was interested more by another subject. "We're dry enough in here, anyhow. Good camp, eh? What about fixin' the primus for a mug of tea? What about them biscuits you told of?"

As with all aborigines, so with Lew comfort and a full belly are of paramount importance. And as it was six o'clock when it was unlikely that Sadie would appear in her dinner hour, Bony agreed, leaving Lew still watching the way down from the cliff.

Partially filling the tank, and attending to the burner with the pricker attached, he obtained rain-water from a rock at the end of the overhang. They munched biscuits and drank tea well laced with sugar as the sea and the great rock withdrew slowly into the night.

Despite the growing storm Bony determined to maintain surveillance of the descent from the top throughout the night hours, not forgetting that Sadie or another had visited this place at night. Thus when Lew fell silent and then yawned, he said they would have to stand watch and that Lew could sleep for the first six hours.

Having made sure there were no traces of their presence, Lew lay down on his blankets in his damp clothes and slept in the complete darkness of the cavern, while Bony sat at the entrance watching and listening to the growing roar of the sea below and the whining of the wind about the rock overhang. He expected nothing to happen, but it did. And he was made happy by the end of boredom.

The torch-beam flickered on the rock-splinters as its owner came carefully down the treacherous descent, now most dangerous in the dark with the heavy surges below. Aided by his own torch he retreated and roused Lew.

"Someone coming. No noise, not a breath. Whatever you see you keep dumb. This could be the job's end."

Lew's response was to kneel beside Bony and with him peer between the saw-teeth of the upthrust rock. The darkness remained with them for a further two minutes, and then with little warning the torch-beam was probing into the entrance. There reached them a low sound. The visitor was humming 'Onward Christian Soldiers'. The visitor came onward too, and the moisture of rain on the oilskin coat was gleaming in the reflected light of the torch.

The figure, looking immense, arrived at the chest. The torch was placed on the chest, and the figure's arms were raised to take down the pressure lamp. And when the lamp was being pumped the springing light revealed Sadie Stark.

They watched her replace the lamp, switch off the torch, and remove her sou'wester and oilskin. She was dressed as a man, and did any set of conditions demand male apparel it was the set ruling this night. From her gunny-sack she took a leather holdall and either a Bible or a Prayer Book; and for minutes she sat on the chest, her face tilted downward in that attitude of still repose never to be forgotten by Bony. When she moved to action she gave a slight shock to the watchers.

Kneeling before the chest, she opened the holdall and from it took an ivory-backed hairbrush and hand-mirror and comb, and proceeded to brush her hair which fell to a surprising length. The light made it shine in its chestnut hue. She began again to hum the hymn, almost crooning a lullaby, as though she delighted in what she was doing.

Neither Bony nor Lew were strangers to a woman combing her hair and putting on her face, but as the minutes passed they witnessed the birth of another woman, a much younger woman in this new hair arrangement, plus the application of powder and lipstick and eye-shadow. Sadie might have done this every day for years, so expert was she.

The two men who long since had lost interest in a woman dressing and only gave a verdict on the completed preparation for a party, were now unable to avoid watching this woman remove all her clothes down to her panties. Standing, she touched the nipples of her breasts with rouge. She took the mirror to examine them better, then to survey her hair and her face, and it seemed many minutes before she was satisfied and removed the toilet articles from the chest in order to raise the lid.

From the sack she took a parcel wrapped in stout paper, and from this a slip, and a pair of nylon stockings. Sitting on the edge of the open chest, she put on the nylons. She reached for the red shoes and put them on. The men, now really interested, saw her stand to slip over her head with expert care the white dress with the polka dots, carefully smooth it into position and be transformed into the young girl of the picture taken at the cricket match.

When she was finished the wide mouth was set in a derisive smile. She made a final check with the mirror, and pirouetted in a dainty way as she might have done in those faraway years in the company of Rose Jukes and the Rhudder boys. The smile vanished, and there appeared vexation in its place and a soft expletive of annoyance broke from her lips.

From the gunny-sack she took two short red candles, and from the chest what looked a steel meat-skewer. She proceeded to the altar rock, passing to stand behind it, and from the iron sticks she removed the candle-butts and placed there the red candles which she lit. On returning to the chest she tossed the butts and the skewer into it, and again surveyed the altar rock.

These actions conforming to theatrical mime would not in themselves have been of interest to Bony if performed by a woman mentally deranged, but Sadie revealed nothing of mental disturbance and no indication of it had been revealed at their previous meetings. She had always appeared to be self-reliant, studious, well-balanced and sometimes introspective as proved by the periods of deep meditation. He was now watching her take up the black-covered book and step forward to stand on the rock-rib at the outer edge of the sand, before the burning candles with the beret between them.

There she made a semi-curtsy, the free hand spreading the frilly skirt. The blazing lamp behind her cast her silhouette against the grey-dark rock wall. She was a stranger to him in these moments. Previously she had appeared to him with her hair tight and her body encased in men's clothes: now her hair was beautiful, and her body was full and free. Every movement portrayed youth, with its restless urge to fly.

Then she was kneeling, facing the altar, and the book was opened and held by both hands, Her face was uplifted as though her gaze was centred at a point high above the beret, and she began to intone from the book which her eyes did not see.

It seemed to Bony that this went on for some time. He could hear her voice but could not distinguish the words, and there was a flatness in the voice indicative of reciting well-remembered passages. When it was ended, the book was set aside, and the girl remained kneeling, but now with her face downward in the old pose of meditation ... or praying.

When Bony felt the coldness in his scalp, he attributed it to the change of wind, to the cold south blowing into the cavern. It was with him when Sadie Stark fell forward on to the sand-patch, fell face down with her arms stretched. He could see her fingers clasping and unclasping, and then taking up sand and tossing it over her head and her white dress.

Lew moved slightly against Bony, and Bony, glancing at him, saw temptation on his face to go forward and try to pacify the girl he had known from her infancy, possibly as he had often done. He placed a restraining hand on Lew's arm, and when Lew looked at him he shook his head.

Sadie's abandonment to grief continued for some time, until it was spent in exhaustion. She lay there a little longer, then rose to her feet and took the beret from the altar. They watched her kneel and scoop a hole in the sand. The beret she placed in the hole. Hesitantly it seemed. She was undecided even to the last whether to inter the beret. Her hands drew the sand over it, covered it, and then, with frantic haste smoothed the place and the marks her body had made.

There followed another period when she stood back from the sand-patch, again in the pose of meditation, and at the close of this phase she stepped quickly to one side, approached the rock at the end, passed behind it to blow out the candles. That done, she came back to the closet.

Sand grains fell from her hair, and she shook her head and freed the hair to cascade again down her back. The make-up was ruined, her face a travesty. The frock was undamaged, and this added to the travesty. She was panting. Her wide mouth was open, and from her eyes tears ran down to furrow the sand caked there by previous tears.

With no regard for the dress, she almost tore it from her and tossed it into the chest. The slip followed, and then the red shoes and the stockings. She did her hair in the usual style, dressed, put the toilet things in the sack, dragged the oilskin into place, and crushed the sou'wester upon her head. The lid of the chest fell with a loud thud. The darkness rushed about her when she extinguished the lamp. The torch-beam accompanied her to the entrance and into the storm raging without.

Bony counted twenty before, with his own torch to guide him, he ran to the entrance and peered round the rock angle to the ledge. The wind striking the cliff-faces was an upward blast. The sea pounded the rocks below in ceaseless cacophony. The torchlight was continuous, and then flickered when the girl's coat beat about her legs. He watched her climb to the top, and was conscious of Lew's closeness to him, while all the aroused sympathy for Sadie Stark's grief slowly ebbed, slowly dried into sand, leaving him cold and desolate of emotion.

"We'll brew a billy of tea," he told Lew. "There's a job we have to do. Get the primus going: I'll fill the billy."

They relit the pressure lamp and Lew attacked the stove while Bony found no difficulty in filling the can at a rock gutter outside. Lew pumped the stove, and had to be told to stop else it might blow up. While they waited for the water to come to the boil, he asked:

"What she bury that beret for?"

"I don't think I know, Lew."

The aborigine's expression was almost comical in its bedevilment.

"What goes, Nat? What goes? Gettin' up in that new dress? Coming down here a night like tonight. Crying like she done, and tossing sand all over herself." Almost pleadingly, he added: "You tell me, eh?"

"We'll soon find out, Lew. Finish your tea."

Afterwards, Bony procured the old shovel and one of the harpoons and Lew accompanied him to the altar. Bony prodded the harpoon into the sand before it, until he found the beret by its resistance. With the shovel he removed the sand and lifted it out and put it back on the altar. Lew grunted and watched him push the harpoon down deeper, and still deeper, until it was stopped by resistance not of the sand. Looking again at Lew, he said:

"Those candlesticks she brought here belong to old Jeff. Missed 'em the other day and went crook, saying Luke took them. Could be that Sadie planted other things from old Jeff down here. We'll soon find out. Put a match to those candles. Give us more light."

"Too right, Nat," agreed poor Lew.

Bony began digging methodically and without haste, and when he had sunk a large excavation of some three feet, he dug more quickly and more horizontally. Soon, thereafter, the edge of the shovel met yielding resistance, and with it Bony scraped slightly to reveal a white blanket. Still more carefully he removed further sand from it, the while Lew stooped above him eager to see what would be disclosed.

Bony tossed aside the shovel and knelt to one side of the blanket. By touch he found the hem and lifted it and gently drew it down. There was revealed a large brown and white shell.

"Hold it, Lew," he cried, and removed the shell.

There was uncovered the face of a man. Over the eyes were small shells of delicate white. The face was large, the skin was yellow-green. Near the summit of the lofty forehead there was a hole edged with black.

Bony whipped back the blanket to reveal the torso covered with a white shirt stained by two small discs of black-dried blood, one under the heart, the other at the right shoulder.

A strangling gurgle broke from Lew. Bony heard him gasp in air.

"Who is he, Lew?" he demanded, looking up into the glaring black eyes. "Tell me who he is. I must know."

The aborigine shrank away, yet was unable to remove his gaze from the dead man. He seemed about to collapse through being unable to draw air into his lungs. Then it came:

"Marvin! Marvin! The Kedic! Arr ... The Kedic Feller." Then Lew sprawled flat in his spring away from the horror. Scrambling to his feet he rushed for the entrance. Bony raced after him, ran through the passage calling on him to stop. On the ledge beyond he was forced to stop himself. He shouted along the ledge, and the blast drove his voice back into his mouth. Once only he heard the cry, thin and distant:

"Kedic, Kedic Feller."

Chapter Twenty-three

Helping Out

He was sorry for Lew, and being sorry was a help in his own need. Standing there with the wind flaying his light clothes and biting with cold into the back of his head and neck, he pressed his face to the rock and waited for the trembling to subside.

It was one of his few weaknesses, this terrible fear of the dead. It was not unlike an un-nameable and un-imagined thing clinging to the very core of his being as a sucker-fish to the skin of a shark, a something which had affixed itself to him before birth, a thing which had existed from the dawn of Man and slunk through a thousand generations to make craven such as he.

The moment the harpoon met yielding obstruction he knew what lay beneath, knew the purpose of the powerful perfume of boronia, but Lew had no suspicion of what that blanket would disclose when pulled aside. Poor Lew! It was a wicked act doing that to him, but none the less it had to be done, the corpse had to be identified after the passage of many days.

Poor old Lew! Just an unoffending elderly man bridging the last of the primitive generations of his race when the first of the new and educated ones, and which, when it passed on, would take with it all the wisdom and the knowledge gained and handed down from man to man squatting over little fires and telling tales of what his eyes had seen. Bony doubted whether in the complete darkness of this night, the aborigine would have made the cliff top.

When the shock subsided, the demands of his long and distinguished career clamoured for attention to the current problems, and now the old pride became a spur to do those tasks he had to do, and the dark shadow of his aboriginal ancestors was pushed aside by the inrush of the white man's logic.

Again in the cavern, he strode to the grave, knelt and replaced the shell over the awful face, and deliberately restraining threatening frenzy, filled in the hole and smoothed the surface. Then blowing out the candles, he sat on the chest and fought again for composure, and even now could not wholly succeed, and blamed the boronia. He washed his hands in kerosene, dried them in the sand, and took the billycan to the water-gutter and, again battling with the cold south wind, felt himself cleansed.

It was when sipping the hot tea and smoking a cigarette that the facts of yet another triumph came to light his mind. He had been given an assignment and he had completed it. He had been asked to find Marvin Rhudder, and he had found him. And once again he could meet his colleagues and square his shoulders. Again he had flirted with failure and had tossed the bitch aside like an old rag.

Well, the news would make the upper Brass happy, and the victims, either dead, or in a lunatic asylum, were avenged. All would say good riddance to the monster, and then to spoil so tidy an end would demand to know who had been the Sir Galahad. Who had killed poor Marvin Rhudder? Who had pumped three bullets into him to make sure he would stay dead? Who had prevented another rendezvous with another victim?

He, Bony, would have to carry on, would have to begin a new investigation and, when he found the blackguard who had foully murdered poor Marvin Rhudder, he could present a double triumph to the many who were envious of his unbroken record.

"Oh! I thought I'd left the light on."

Sadie Stark stood at the inner end of the long entrance. Water streamed from her coat and sou'wester. The rain had washed her face and the wind had massaged it to bring up the vivid colour. Bony stood:

"Hullo, Sadie! Come along in and have a mug of tea. You look wet, and must feel cold and tired. Let me help you with your coat."

Her eyes were wide and steady upon him. Momentarily they gazed at the altar, and she must have seen the beret left on it.

She let him take the oilskin and the sou'wester which he placed on a rocky spur, and at his invitation she sat on the chest and accepted the mug of tea to which he added sugar, without asking. Wisely, he was patient with her.

He brought the water-tin, now empty, and sat on that before her. He rolled a cigarette, offered it to her and she declined. The colour was gone from her face now, and her lips, at first compressed, now softened and began faintly to tremble.

"How long have you been here, Nat?" she asked, the shock of finding him yet upon her.

"For some time, Sadie. Why did you come back? On a night like this, too?"

"I can see you found the beret. I came back to bury something else with it."

"Did you, indeed! Must be important. Anyway, let it wait. I'll go for more water, and we'll boil the billy again."

Almost casually he picked up the can and sauntered to the entrance. He passed into the storm and groped his way to the gushing water-gutter, where he filled the billy, and took it back. He half expected to find her with the automatic taken from the chest, the cartridges from which were in his pocket. The behaviour pattern would set his own. Sadie Stark was still seated on the chest, her head low and her gaze fixed upon her feet.

"Does the sea ever come high enough to wash into this cavern?" he asked, as he pumped the primus.

"It must have done at one time. Long ago. Before we found this cavern. It's coming high now and we'll have to wait till past high tide before we can get back to the cliff. I only just made it."

"It can't be far off daylight. Where's your torch?"

"I slipped outside and dropped it. It fell down the rocks."

"Eat a biscuit or two." She accepted, and then looked up at him, and when she spoke her voice was low and sad.

"Who are you, Nat? What are you?"

"I'm only a policeman, Sadie. And Nat is as good as another name. What did you want to bury with the beret?"

"An old album. It doesn't matter now. Did you watch when I was being very dramatic and silly?"

"Yes. I couldn't turn my eyes away. My job is to find Marvin Rhudder, and when I came here and saw his beret on the rock there, I was sure he'd been here. Of course, I knew you'd been here, often. Then I found what could well be his pistol in the chest. Is it?"

Sadie nodded, raised the mug to her lips and looked unwaveringly over it at him.

"Yes, he forgot to take it away with him. Like the beret."

Bony nodded as though he understood and accepted this simple statement.

"I remember you telling me in confidence that Marvin came home, and his parents had to call for Luke to come down and get rid of him. It was the morning we caught the kingfish, the morning the sneaker very nearly caught me. You know, sometimes I think you delayed to warn me so that the sneaker would get me. Why?"

The girl's eyes opened with astonishment, and colour mounted in her face.

"Waited to warn you, that you would be drowned? Oh, Nat, you can't think that of me. I was at fault, terribly so. But I didn't fail deliberately. I ... You see, I couldn't get Marvin out of my mind. I couldn't stop thinking about him."

"I am very glad to hear that Sadie. I didn't like thinking ill of you, and you must forgive me for doing so. Tell me, on the day we fished, did you know that Marvin was dead?"

The lamp suspended above and behind her shed its glare full upon him, and, instead of replying, Sadie continued to regard him as she might regard a rare shell to be added to her collection. She almost came to studying him; careful to note the black straight hair greying at the temples, the straight thin nose and the mobile lips above the strong chin. Then she looked long and hard at his forehead, and the frontal bone which did not shadow the blue eyes beneath. Her gaze encountered his, and she could observe nothing in his eyes save kindliness, and what seemed to be pleading.

"Yes," she whispered, nodding. "Yes, I knew he was dead that day. It's why I forgot you and the sneaker."

"Who killed him? Luke?"

"No. I killed him."

The admission was made with such frankness and lack of emotion that Bony was halted in his mental tracks, and took time off to roll a cigarette. Requiring additional time, he strolled to the entrance and smoked the cigarette without noticing that the roof of the world was turning grey. On going in he found Sadie as he had left her, and again sitting on the water-tin, he said:

"This is most serious. You realize it, I suppose?"

She nodded.

"Was it you who buried him?"

She caught her breath and expelled it in a long drawn-out sigh. Raising her head to look again directly at him, he saw on her face the mysterious, wistful, haunting, smile, and at first it made him feel rising indignation, and then looking deeply into her unmasked eyes he understood that this expression was a front, merely a front to conceal a dictated retirement to isolation, giving the only sanctuary from fear and hurt.

"Don't answer that question yet," he told her. "Let me tell you something. I'm a detective-inspector. I told you I've a wife and three sons. I've apprehended many criminals. I came to the Inlet to apprehend Marvin Rhudder. I've been told often that I am a sentimental ass, for more than once I have ended a case feeling deep sympathy for the man or the woman I've had to arrest.

"Now I have to arrest you for the murder of Marvin Rhudder. I have to warn you that anything you say henceforth I may take down in writing and use it against you. I don't want to do either the one or the other, but we are both subject to the Law. Now: did you bury him?"

"Yes. Oh, Nat!" She had to fight to maintain control. "Yes, I buried him. I put him in the grave over there. I washed the blood from his face and covered his eyes with small shells and his face with a large one. I buried the beret because it was his, and I came back to bury the album because everything in it belongs to him. There were other things of his in a suitcase, and I planted that in a hollow tree I intended one day to set fire to."

"Why did you put the suitcase in the hollow tree?"

"He lived in a hut near a paperbark swamp because there was water there, and no one ever went there excepting to muster the cattle. When Luke came down he tried to get him to go away, telling him he'd broken his father's heart and was breaking his mother's heart by hiding on their land. I was taking food to him, and when he said he was on the run because he'd broken bond, I was against sending him away. You see, I still loved him. It didn't seem to make any difference what he'd done to Rose Jukes, to those other women and the man who went mad, and the little children: it didn't make any difference what he'd done to old Jeff and his mother and to me. He came back older in looks and yet as splendid as when he went away.

"The day before he went away there was a cricket match in Timbertown, and we all went to it, and afterwards in the garden he told me he loved me so much, and we would marry immediately he was ordained. And when he came back, after all the terrible years, I forgot everything he'd done, and went on loving him.

"And so I took food to him, and a few books, cooked meals there at the hut. Luke told him to get to hell off the place, and I told him behind Luke's back to stay on and we'd find a good cave where he'd be safe. He stayed, and then one day the Senior came to say the police in South Australia were wanting him for murder. Luke and I went that night and told him the Senior had been and why. He told Marvin that if he didn't clear out he would tell the Senior where he was. Marvin flew into one of his rages and Luke knocked him down, and took me back home.

"I pleaded with Luke to give him one more chance to go, before telling the Senior. Luke gave me money and I took what I had, and some his mother gave too. I went to Marvin to tell him it was his last chance. There he was lying on the floor of the hut, his face like paper, shaking all over, even his teeth chattering. And what was the matter with him was fright, fright of being hanged for murder.

"I couldn't send him away, Nat. How could I? I brought him here, and afterwards took him food and water. He felt safe here, because no one knew about it excepting us Rhudders and Ted Jukes, and Ted was dead. After a little while Marvin got better, and then he remembered his suitcase; it wasn't there. He said it could only be back at the hut, and I agreed to fetch it after dark, because if I met Matt or Karl they'd want to know what I was doing with it.

"And then after what happened that day, the same day, I felt I couldn't bring it here. I felt ... So I took it to the hollow tree and dropped it in there. I thought I was careful with it too. I sponged the case inside and out with a wet rag, and I carried it by a rag round the handle."

Bony went again to the entrance to ponder and was appalled by what the new day revealed. On returning, he said: "Why the hurricane lamp?"

"I brought it for Marvin. When he complained about the poor light, I brought the pressure lamp, and left the hurricane in case my torch failed."

"Simple. Well, as it appears we'll be here for hours, let's get on with the story. You say that Marvin missed his suitcase left behind at the hut. You promised to go for it after dark. All that is clear and in order. What follows is in order too. Because you wouldn't go for the case before dark, and he knew there was a great deal of money in it he'd want for his getaway, he became moody, and the mood became insane rage. Right?"

"Yes. He did fly into a rage. And then ..."

"It's quite clear as to what followed. His automatic pistol with other things were lying on the chest. Correct?"

Sadie nodded, slightly bewildered.

"In the storm of his fury he made a grab for you, and you could see terrible things in his eyes and on his face. You turned and ran, but he blocked your escape at the entrance. You told him what you thought of him after all you'd done to help him, and he came for you again. Correct?"

"Yes. No, it wasn't like ..."

"It was, Sadie. You know it was. He came for you in a wild rush and you ran behind the chest and you saw the automatic, and in your fear and desperation you snatched up the weapon and fired at him. Now didn't you? In your extremity, you snatched up the pistol and fired at him."

"Yes. Yes, Nat. No, it wasn't... . Stop making me say things I don't mean."

His eyes grew big and as deep as the deep blue sea. He shouted at her: "I'm not making you say anything, Sadie. I'm saying it for you."

Chapter Twenty-four

At High Tide

The eye of the wind, having circled towards the Antarctic, had worked on the sea with spectacular results. The Front Door of Australia was now being savaged by all the white ghosts from the South, tearing at the feet of the monolith, leaping high as though to clutch the hair of a giant and pull him down for the lesser attackers to devour.

Waves and rollers there were none, for the white hills of water rushing in behind the Door, there to meet and rise to mountainous summits, could not be likened to waves. You could count slowly fifty seconds from the appearance of one range at each edge of the Door until the appearance of the next. Having entered behind the Door, they proceeded as the spokes of a wheel, curving against the tall rock faces of the cliffs in white masses, ultimately to meet and struggle opposite where Bony stood with Sadie under the overhang. Every half-minute or thereabouts, the rocks at the beach level were boiled black, and half a minute later the level of the tortured 'snowfield' was less than ten feet below the ledge where they were standing.

The sky appeared to be resting on the top of the Door and it appeared also to be taking to itself the colour of the sea to make it French-grey. The wind was cold, and showed its velocity when whipping off great masses of suds and rushing them up the cliff-faces and over into the tea-tree. The ledge under the overhang gave almost a vacuum, so that these masses of suds flew up and past them like bed sheets whisked off a line by a twister.

That section of the ledge which joined the rock over which they would have to clamber to reach the upward path, was smothered at the apex of each water-hill. Having repeatedly counted the seconds from one flood to the following one, Bony calculated they could reach the rock provided they hastened for it and provided they did not slip on wetted rock pavements. To run would be hardly possible.

To hear on this exposed ledge what either might say would be impossible too, and he motioned Sadie to retreat with him into the cavern.

"D'you know when high tide is due?"

"No," replied the girl. "I would have, had I seen the sun rise."

"I've been studying those waves, and if they rise much higher we'll be cut off. What d'you think?"

"Even if the tide is on the ebb, the wind won't let it fall. The waves could rise so high as to wash into this cavern and drown us. I wish it would. I want to die. I don't want to go on living. So let me be."

They were standing near the hurricane lamp where the daylight served them. Bony moved fractionally to gain position between Sadie and the sea. She stood there looking at his feet, seemingly demure but actually lost in a world of dark despair. When he spoke again his voice was raised to biting anger, and there can be no doubt that what he said and how he said it would have merited his Marie's approval.

"You don't want to live any more. You want to die. What bloody rot! You stand there moaning and wringing your hands like that fool Othello after he'd strangled Desdemona. Your heart, your mind, every part of you, is weeping over a Thing. Blast your eyes! I've a good mind to slap it out of you." With one hand he gripped her arm, and with the other roughly forced her chin upward, only to see her eyes closed. "Now let me tell you this, stupid. Thirteen, fourteen years ago you were a simpering, dreamy-eyed, fool of a female child in love with a great big Knight arrayed in Shining Mail. Your own words. And the truth. Your Knight in Shining Mail went off to capture a dream for you, and a Dragon killed him. A Dragon! What an insult to a dragon."

Still Sadie wouldn't look at him. He shook her, and went on with the verbal thrashing:

"All you've had to cling to, like a limpet to a rock, was a vision of a Knight in Shining Mail. And don't call me a liar. D'you hear? You've been in love all these years with a vision, and when this Marvin came slinking back you kidded yourself he was still the knight you created. When Marvin proved to you, and the proof I'll get out of you before I'm through, when he proved to you that he wasn't the substance of your Glorious Vision of Love you shot him, shot a Thing, not the Vision."

Sadie's eyes opened wide. They were steady in dazed wonderment, in puzzled astonishment, and he sensed it was not because of what he was saying but of the manner of saying it. He despaired of getting through to her, yet persevered.

"Your Knight in Shining Mail has been just a disguise you put around poor bloody Marvin. You shoved it on: he didn't put it on. Most every woman in her secret heart has the vision of the Knight. My Marie's always had it. Every time Emma looks at her Matt, I've seen she too has the vision of Love. You're nothing out of the ordinary, you silly bitch. You're damn lucky to have had it and still have it. And you are going to meet a man some day on whom you can put the disguise, and find him able to wear it. It won't fit properly, of course, because no man could possibly wear well the magic suit you women weave and make." He shook her again. "You listening to me?"

"You're rather wonderful, Nat," she said, and Bony gasped.

"Wonderful be damned! Oh, my tragic aunt! I've been ramming common-sense down your throat and you say I'm wonderful. Now you get going along that ledge and up the cliff, not down. Are you going to be difficult? Am I to handcuff you to me? Or what? Go on! Go on! Answer me."

"I promise not to commit suicide, Nat, if that's what you fear."

"I fear nothing of the kind. If I did, I'd clip you under the chin and carry you up the cliff on a shoulder. No one suicides on me, or not often. No. You've got to come out of that Alice in Wonderland world of yours. You've got to be your age. Ahead of you are sticky patches, and a few dark places, but you are going to be all right because you have with you all along the road your old pal, Nat. Now let's get out of this joint."

Again on the ledge, Bony urged Sadie forward and out from the overhang. He had foreseen the obstacle of her oilskin and had said nothing as the rain had stopped. They became at once the sport of the strong uprush of air carrying the masses of sea-suds. They proceeded as far as the waves had left untouched, and this was some hundred feet from the junction rock.

Sadie looked back to Bony, and saw the sud-mass wrap itself about his head, causing him to dig it from his face and out of his eyes. Another mass hit her back, and the lip of a white wave came to her feet. As it began to recede he waved her forward and she began to run.

The path, roughly horizontal here with the beach, sank a little towards the goal. There were short stretches of sand on which Bony had first seen her tracks, and these stretches were separated by rock-bars and slivers of rock and pebbles. The girl was wearing sand-shoes, having serrated rubber soles, and the advantage was with her as Bony's shoes were of leather. Reaching the rock, she clambered upward to its summit, perhaps ten feet higher in elevation, and on glancing backward saw Bony on hands and knees.

The next wave was on its course, and she screamed at him to hurry. He could see the wave engulfing the beach rocks, could look down at its terrifying maw and the vast body of white water humped behind it. He flung himself forward, slipped and recovered his balance, and reached the rock at the instant his feet were trapped.

Then Sadie was hanging head downward like a lobster to its crevice, one hand gripping Bony's wrist. The wave swept his feet from under. It buried him to his shoulders, raised him to Sadie's level. For an age it seemed he clung to the rock with one hand and felt Sadie's grip about his other wrist. He did nothing to resist the subsequent drag and, the wave retreating, regained his feet and climbed to the girl's side.

At the cliff top, he said:

"Where would I have been now had you determined to die? Come on, pal. There's music to face."

Among the tea-tree clumps it was almost calm. Sadie retrieved her gunny-sack from a branch where she had left it, and side by side they went down the slope to the Inlet. Bony said:

"One day Matt and I were talking up here, and someone tried to overhear what we were saying. Who was it, d'you know? Luke or Marvin?"

"Luke. He told me about it. He suspected you from the first. I did, too. But as Marvin was dead, I thought I had nothing to fear from you."

"You haven't. From me."

In one of its many moods the sea had shredded the seaweed-mountain and had nudged its soggy masses past the Inlet sand-wall, and on towards Australia's Front Door. The Door had refused to admit it. The irritated sea had taken it back. The angry sea had rebuilt the weed into a mountain opposite the Inlet sand-bar. Now the furious sea was beating upon it, surging over it and about it, making no impression on the spongy mass. The sea had built a Door of its own, only to find in its blind temper that its Door was as impervious to its onslaught as the great rock Door had been for centuries.

As happened behind Australia's Front Door, here, too, the sea was rushing in behind its seaweed mountain, and with each tremendous surge was carrying thick slices off the front of the sand-bar. The width of the great wall was now but a fraction of what it had once been.

"Doesn't look so good," Bony shouted to conquer the wind. "There's strangers at the homestead, too."

Outside the garden-gate was a group of horsemen. One held the reins of a horse ridden by the man talking to people on the house veranda. Even at this distance and in the light of this angry day, they could see among the group two aborigines. The man below the veranda came hastening to the party, and on taking the reins of his horse, vaulted into the saddle and led his companions at a canter to the sea wall.

"We'd better hurry if we want to cross," shouted Sadie.

Bony brought his mouth closer to her, and she failed to understand him when he said:

"We don't want to cross to the homestead. It's too late now, anyway.

Look at this one coming in."

By comparison the sneaker was a dwarf. It rushed upon the seaweed mountain. The wind seemed to lift from its summit vast masses of water, only to send them chasing after the parent-body, and to arrive at the obstacle at the identical moment. The enormous wave rose to fall upon the enemy, to bury it and frenziedly struggle to strangle it. It raced in behind the victim to fall upon the sand-wall, to churn and tear at it, finally to stand back as though to observe the effects. It might not have liked what it saw, for it began hurriedly to bypass the still triumphant seaweed mountain and retreat to the reinforcement racing shoreward.

The Inlet now took over. It burst the weakened sand-wall. It flung the seaweed mountain from its path. It roared over the remains, and in black solidity chased the retreating white wave to catch it just before it met the next incoming water range. It rode high over all opposition, drove a mighty black wedge into the white ocean. It tore the remainder of the sandbar from its foundations. It knifed slices off the opposite sand-dune, and it ate into the solid earth below Bony and the girl, flicking rocks off their iron bases and making the ground shudder. Although safe, they stepped slowly backward and up the slope, unable to remove their gaze from the spectacle of the imprisoned power suddenly released.

"It's terrific! Just terrific!" Sadie kept shouting, and Bony was conscious of her arm being slipped under his, and his arm pressing it against his side. He thought grimly that where he might have failed in the cavern, this event was knocking some common-sense into her.

Over on the far side, Sasoon waved to them. Bony saw him shouting but was unable to hear above the roar of the released Inlet. Two were strangers to him, but he recognized Matt and Breckoff and Fred and Lew. Mark Rhudder was running from the homestead, and old Jeff was standing with Sarah at the garden-gate. Already the shore was draped with an ever-widening ribbon of black mud as the water receded.

The boat would be already useless in its shelter shed. Bony was glad that they would have to walk around the west side of the dying Inlet and so on to Matt's homestead, instead of being able to cross and confront old Jeff and his wife with Sadie's detention, and the reason for it.

"We'll have to walk round to Matt's house," he told Sadie. "Sasoon and those with him will meet us somewhere. After last night's deluge cars and trucks will be impossible for a couple of days. Come on, let's start."

Turning to walk up the slope, the girl would have withdrawn her arm so impulsively slipped under his, but it was held captive.

Chapter Twenty-five

The Man at the Helm

Sadie had once read a detective book Emma had given her, and the detective had said to the murderer: "Come, take a little walk with me." This must be what Nat was doing right now.

Presently she espied among other trees that old hollow one in which she had dropped Marvin's case, and she asked how he had found it.

"Just followed your tracks, Sadie."

"But. ... But, I smoothed them out with a branch. I made sure."

"You did so. You changed your footprints to leaf prints. Next time you think to fool your old pal, do it just before a good rain."

He compelled a halt in the lee of a tree, and released her arm to roll a cigarette. He offered to make her one but again she declined. The wind sang through the branches, and now the clouds were being blown to pieces and the sun was due to take command. When going on, he took her hand in his. They were able to move more easily. She said, without attempting to pull away:

"I won't try to escape, Nat."

"Escape from me, no. And I shall not permit you to escape from yourself any more. You've been doing that for years, trying to escape from yourself." They stood for a few moments looking at the Inlet already shrunk to half its original area, and bordered by ever widening strips of mud. "It will look very ugly until the grass grows and covers it all up. Now come on, and if you'd rather not have me hold your hand, I'll oblige."

Then she was free and walking in step, and he said:

"You see, Sadie, I know much about you because before I met and married my Marie, I was lonely, too. I know what it is to live always alone with myself, having no one to be close to, having to travel always on a one-way street. I had my studies, but they didn't really help. At present you are walking into a great deal of trouble and anxiety. You will be subject to constraint because us poor policemen have to follow routine laid down by our betters. You won't like the publicity. You will be asked countless questions, by police officers, court officials and lawyers.

"You will feel battered, but I believe you will stand up to it because you have for long been introverted. I'm game to bet you haven't laughed properly for years. Anyway, presently we shall be met by Sasoon and others, and I shall have to commit you to them, and you will be arrested and eventually charged with murder. I am doubtful how far the law will go. I won't be able to be with you, you know, to keep you in order and threaten to smack you if you don't behave."

Glancing at him, she noted his strong profile, and straight hair whipped by the wind, the old clothes he was wearing in that way where mufti cannot disguise the soldier. The odd thing about him was that he made her feel she had known him all her life. He was saying:

"You'll be staying with Emma for a day or two, and I'll have someone ride down to the homestead for the things you'll want. Then I'll have you make a statement covering all that has happened, and get you to sign it before witnesses. Will you remember something?"

"I shall never forget anything, Nat."

"Oh yes, you will, eventually. But remember this, and it's important. Don't answer any questions put to you by anyone about what has happened before I take your statement. Clear?"

Sadie replied by clasping his hand and pressing it. Minutes later, he said:

"Ah! Now, chin up! Here they are."

Emma placed on a tray two cups of tea, sugar, a plate of buttered scones, with a dish of her own strawberry jam. She carried the tray from the living-room to a bedroom where the lace curtains were trembling before the open french windows, and to which had been added two easy chairs and a table. Putting the tray on the table, she sat and looked at Sadie Stark.

"They got Sam's car out of the bog, but you have to stay on here till tomorrow." Emma offered one of the cups to Sadie and Sadie accepted, faintly smiling. "I'm bursting with curiosity, but I've promised not to ask a single question except to ask if you want anything."

"But you can answer my questions. They didn't tell you not to, did they?"

"No, they didn't."

"Where's Nat?"

"He's gone down to talk to your mother and old Jeff. He will be bringing the things you need. Sam and the doctor, and Mr Lang, the magistrate, are over in the barn as far as I know, dear. Lew and Fred are sitting outside in the sun, and Tom Breckoff took off his coat and is giving Karl a hand with the milking."

For Emma it was not unlike looking after an invalid, and secretly she loved it. Sadie had been told by Sasoon that she must not leave the room unless accompanied by Emma, and, if she gave her promise, the windows could be left open and the door to the living-room left ajar. Emma had once heard her crying, but much of the time Sadie spent in meditation.

It was the day following that terrible day of storm which wrecked beautiful Rhudder's Inlet, and it was thought that the track to Timbertown would carry wheel traffic the next day. Matt had volunteered to use horses in a sled to fetch the body of Marvin Rhudder on which Coroner Lang had held a preliminary inquiry, and accepted the depositions from several persons, proving identity. Old Jeff wanted his son buried on the cliff behind Australia's Front Door, but this the law would not permit.

Later, when Emma was cooking dinner for her large official party and her two men, Sadie heard Bony saying to Emma that he had brought the clothes, and perhaps Sadie might like to change into them at once. He said nothing of what had transpired at the homestead, and shortly left the living-room. It was some time after she had eaten dinner in her room that Bony asked to come in.

"I've come to ask questions to fill in the blanks so that your statement can be prepared," he told her, and the door appeared to be closed by the draught from the windows. "Had a restful day?"

"Yes, Nat."

"Good! Then we'll rough out this statement, and in the morning I'll read it over to you and have you sign it. You haven't forgotten what I said about not signing another one?"

"Oh, Nat, I've forgotten nothing you've ever said."

"Well, you forget about those swear-words. Now let's to the job."

In mid-morning the next day, Constable Breckoff asked her to come to the living-room, and there she found Bony seated at the table with Sasoon. They both stood. There was no welcoming smile. They were stiff in attitude, and Bony spoke crisply:

"Good morning, Sadie. Please take this chair. Thank you. Now I have here ... you needn't stand behind Miss Stark, Constable. Sit down. I have before me the many statements you have made to me, which I have incorporated into a concise document. I will read it to you, and should there be anything you wish deleted, or added, you must at once say so. Understood?"

Sadie inclined her head, and for a moment he thought she was going to fall into habit. However, she looked up again and continued to regard him as he prepared to read. He was so different from the Nat Bonnar she had known. He was dressed in a smart grey suit, and was wearing a grey-striped shirt and collar with a maroon tie. His voice was clipped, and his expression stern.

The statement began with finding Marvin in the shed, and his declaration that he was on the run for breaking his bond. It went on to tell of a conference between him and his mother and Sadie, and their refusal to let him stay at the house because of old Jeff's constantly repeated threat. Late that night, Sadie took him across the Inlet in the boat to the old hut at the paperbark swamp, and the next day Mrs Rhudder wired for Luke. Luke came and told his brother to clear out. The police came asking for Marvin whom they thought had committed a murder, and this caused Luke to repudiate his brother and threaten to inform the police if he did not at once leave.

The statement went on to tell of Sadie's night trips to the hut with food and necessities and of her pleading with him to go away for his sick father's sake. She said how she had found Marvin one morning almost in collapse with fear of being caught and eventually tried and hanged, and of how she had in the end agreed to let him go to the cavern where she continued to succour him, yet continued to urge him to go away.

Such was his state of mind he did not realize he had left in the hut the suitcase he had brought with him, and when she took food and water to him it was after a stormy scene with Luke who agreed to delay informing the police for another twenty-four hours. He did not approve of her succouring Marvin any more, after the scene in the hut when Marvin began to go berserk and Luke knocked him down.

Returning to the suitcase, Sadie said it would be foolish to go for it in broad daylight, but Marvin insisted, and she was obstinate on the ground that she might be seen with it. He had then lost his temper altogether and sprang at her. She had eluded him and managed to get to the back of the chest. He was terrifying and she feared for her life, and on the chest was his pistol which she snatched up and fired at him. She didn't remember how many times she shot him.

The next day she returned to the cavern which had been an old-time pirates' cave when they were all children together. With an old shovel she dug the grave there and placed him in it. It was because of the long relationship, and of her strong affection for the Rhudders that she had put shells on the eyes and a larger one over the face, and had taken candles to burn there and pray for his soul as no one could call the minister. The dress in the chest she had worn to perform that last act. The suitcase she had hidden in the hollow tree. She had not examined the contents, knowing that Marvin would no longer need them. She had returned to bury the album with the beret and find Nat Bonnar there, who was now known to her as Detective Inspector Bonaparte.

Laying down the last sheet, Bony slowly shuffled them into sequence. Sasoon was staring grimly at his hands. Breckoff was frowning, and quite suddenly smiled at Sadie.

"That is your statement, Miss Stark," Bony said, looking up at her. "Is there anything you wish to delete or add?"

Sadie shook her head.

"Then you will sign it?"

Sadie indicated that she would.

They watched her initial every page and write her signature on the last one. Each of them added his initials and signed as witnesses to her signature. Tom Breckoff wrote his as he might in a marriage register. Bony stood, and they stood with him. To Sasoon, Bony said gravely:

"That is my case, Senior. You will take over."

"Passing the buck, sir. All right! Sadie Stark, I arrest you for the murder of one Marvin Rhudder." Sadie swayed a little, looked appealingly at Bony. She seemed unaware that Breckoff was patting her shoulder. She watched Sasoon stride to the telephone and ring a number. Sasoon said:

"That you, Else? Line must be still crook. Hear me? Well, I'm bringing in a prisoner. Leaving at once. Have a room prepared for Sadie Stark. Yes, Sadie Stark. What's that? A cell? Cell be damned, Else. She can have the second bedroom. If I had my way I'd have the ruddy town band out to meet her."

Chapter Twenty-six

The Motive

For Emma Jukes the morning had been heavy with emotion after two days of great excitement, and she felt the need for the peace and quiet of her room to recover the mundane way of life which normally ruled One Tree Farm. She had grieved for Sadie. She had wanted to kiss Sam Sasoon. And now she wanted to take this Nat Bonnar apart and put him into a special niche for future reference.

Bony was still engaged on his reports when Emma entered the living-room. She was dressed in her usual neat afternoon fashion, her dark hair parted in the middle and arranged in that mode of severity which enhanced her femininity. Seeing her, Bony pushed his papers from him and stood to offer her a chair at the table.

"Sit down, Emma, please. I have something to say to you before Matt and Karl come in for dinner. My writing is nearly done, and afterwards I'll help you with the dinner, if you like. It's been nice of you to let me stay on for another day."

"One cook is enough in this house, Nat," she said, on being seated opposite him. "What will happen to Sadie?"

"It's my opinion that the Crown Prosecutor might decline to move against her, and that she will be discharged after the magisterial hearing. She will have to carry her cross that far. It is about Sadie I wish to speak." Bony regarded Emma steadily. "You and Matt know as much about this Marvin Rhudder affair as do Sam and Breckoff, but because you are a wise woman, there is something else I think you should know. For Sadie's good, it is a secret which I feel you'll readily lock in your heart and throw away the key. Will you listen?"

"Of course, Nat."

"I've no doubt that when Sadie's trouble is over she'll find her home again at the Inlet, but she will need so much more than that. Although a grown woman she'll need ... what shall I say? Yes, she'll need mothering. Am I expressing it correctly?"

Emma nodded slowly, saying:

"I've known for years that Sadie wanted just that, that she has never been close to her mother. She seemed always alone. Our Ted knew it, and I think that's why he wanted to marry her. Trust me, Nat."

"I spoke to Sadie in her room just before they left," Bony explained. "I said: 'There's something on your mind, Sadie, which will always be a nuisance until you get rid of it by telling someone about it. I can guess what it is. In fact, I'm reasonably sure that I know. But to free your mind you must tell it to someone. Why not me?'

"She sobbed a little. She clung to me, and I knew then how much she had been starving for understanding affection.

"Sadie was deeply in love with Marvin. Marvin promised to marry her after he was ordained. He promised it the evening before leaving with your Rose for the train to Perth. Long before then she had created a suit of shining mail for him, and despite all the crimes he committed, she continued to regard him as her Knight in Shining Mail. When on her trips to collect shells, she would talk to him. When in the boys' cavern, with the chest opened and the dreadful record being added to, she would discuss his failings. During thirteen years and a bit, Emma.

"We know what her reactions were to his return, and what she did to succour him. Sometimes he was as he used to be, gay, witty, teasing. At other times he was despondent, fearful, and sunk in a pit of self-pity. She was tortured by two loyalties: loyalty to old Jeff, and loyalty to her Knight, her splendid Knight.

"I'm coming to the climax, Emma, and with reluctance. There was Marvin refusing to leave the safety of the cavern. There was Sadie overwhelmed by the vision of love which had been her very existence for all the years since both were young. For Jeff's sake she implored him to go away. She ached to comfort him. She placed her arms about him when he wept, and told him of her love which had so faithfully endured. She went to even greater efforts. She offered to go with him, to be his eyes and ears in the flight from justice. She went still farther. She lay before him when he was sitting on the chest, offering herself as, in her own words, an abandoned woman.

"He sat on the chest, leaning forward, looking at her, and the shining mail was dissolved in the acid bath of his sneering contempt. He said: 'You're no good to me, Sadie. My women have to be hard to get.'

"Marvin stood and turned casually about to go to the tin of water she had lugged all the way from the homestead in the middle of the night. Sadie rose and dressed. The pistol was on the chest. That she slipped her finger off the trigger after her third shot will always astound me."

More from
Arthur Upfield

Other Titles by Arthur W. Upfield and published by ETT Imprint:

Upfield's own drawing of Bony

First time Published

BEYOND THE MIRAGE

An Autobiography

Originally written in 1937, Upfield's own story of
life in England, and travelling around Australia
with his camels, working the Rabbit Proof Fence,
and his encounters with Snowy Rowles. A big
book, heavily illustrated with photographs from
the Upfield family archives. First published
by ETT Imprint, Exile Bay, world-wide in 2020.

Printed in the USA
CPSIA information can be obtained
at www.ICGtesting.com
LVHW051954121223
766150LV00011B/403